# PRINCESS AND THE PAUPER

ISABELLE KELLY

A Wild Ink Publishing Original
wild-ink-publishing.com



ISBN: 978-1-964885-11-7

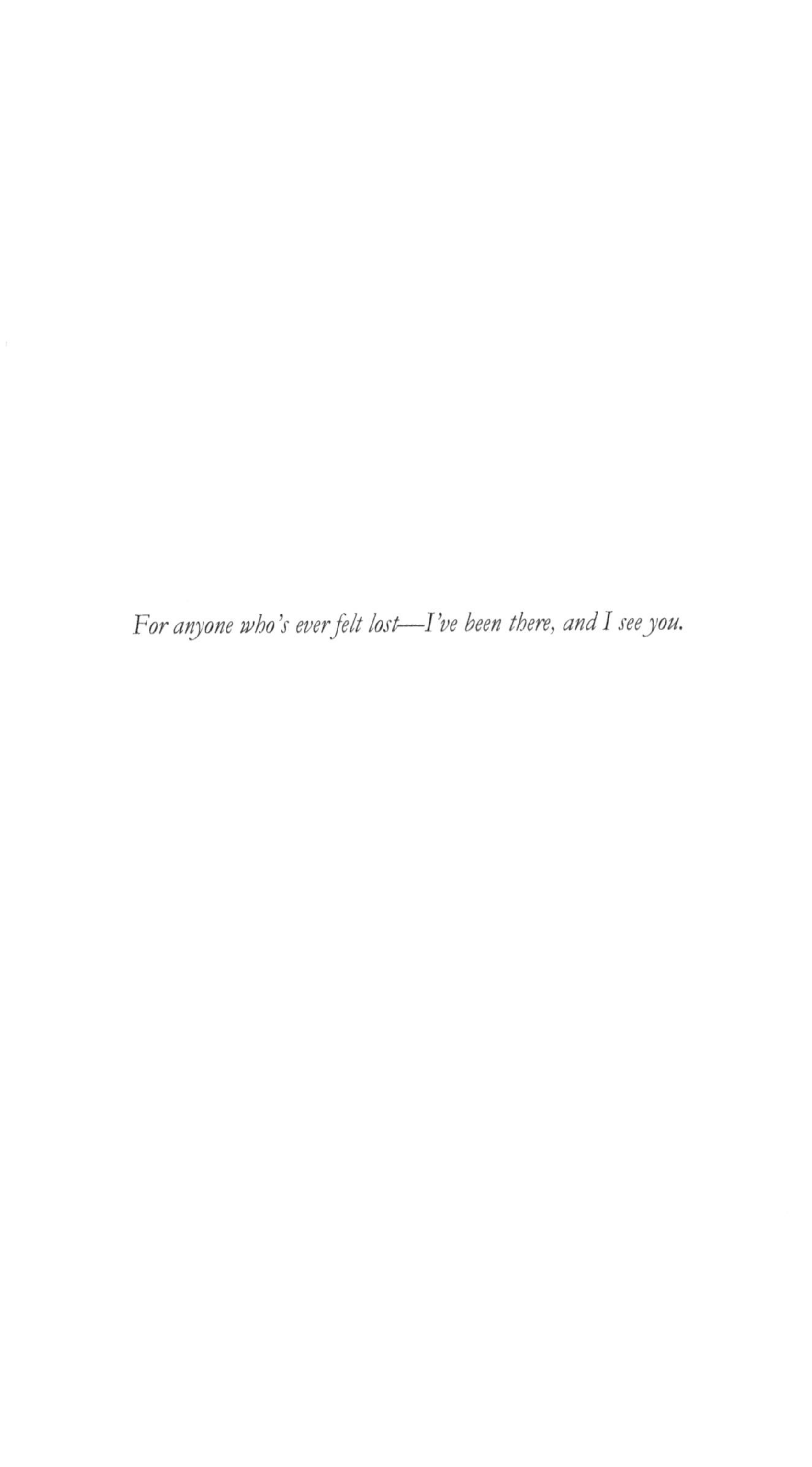
*For anyone who's ever felt lost—I've been there, and I see you.*

# CHAPTER ONE
# AISLING

I'VE NEVER BEEN IN A LINEN closet before. I didn't have time for games like hide-and-seek as a child; my games were more of the *how many capitals of various countries can you memorize?* variety. Being the crown princess of Vyctorya meant that I was destined to live a different life, and in that life, I didn't hide away in linen closets.

The closet is dark, only the faintest bit of light shining through the lip at the bottom of the door. Nonetheless, I can still see Hope's eyes—crystalline blue, clear and bright like the sky and luminescent in the dark of the closet. I wonder what she thinks of my eyes—hazel, leaning more toward brown.

"Are you sure about this?" Hope asks nervously. She leaves off my title, but only because I've begged her to over the past two months she's worked at the palace. Really, I'd asked her to call me by my name—Aisling—but she'd adamantly refused.

"Yes," I say, "but only if you want to."

It's hard to make out Hope's expression in the faint light, but the steady warmth of her palm cups my cheek. Her thumb finds the corner of my mouth and rubs, almost subconsciously.

"You're so sweet," she says, voice soft and low.

I fight a grimace. I don't want pity, and I don't think Hope means it that way, but it always feels a little uneven. Like I like her more than she likes me.

Of course, this isn't a relationship. It can't be. Hope seems to know that better than me. She's never tried to push us past the conversations and light touches. I'd seen the dating apps on her phone when she showed me her home screen picture of her childhood cat.

"Hey." Hope's voice makes me start. My eyes find hers. "You with me?"

"Yes." I lean my cheek into her hand. Her palm is soft, but her fingers are rough, hardened from labor. I wonder what she thinks of my hands. "Please."

And for a moment, everything stops. Hope's eyes are trained on mine as she leans forward slowly. Her breath smells minty and is cool when it hits my skin, leaving goosebumps. As she closes the distance between us, I can make out the curve of her lips, upturned into a slight smile. Her hand tilts my face, and I let my eyes flutter closed.

And then—

"Florence!" It's my mother's voice. I stiffen, and Hope freezes. "Have you seen Aisling?"

"No, Your Majesty." Florence, my lady-in-waiting, is the epitome of calm despite lying through her teeth to her queen. Florence knows exactly where I am. She must have been making a lap when my mother caught her.

"I'm going to call her," Mum says. My eyes widen and I fumble for my phone.

Where is it? *Where* is it?

"Have you checked her room?" Florence asks, voice still as calm as the duck pond behind the palace. I can't hear even a hint of nervousness. Meanwhile, my heart is in my throat, my hands shaking as I wait for the shrill ringing to give me away.

"Oh." Mum pauses. "No, I haven't. I'll ask her if she's there."

"Aisling never remembers her phone," Florence says, stopping my mother once more. "I can go check her room if you'd like?"

There's silence for a moment. I can picture my mum's face, lips pursed and eyebrows furrowed as she thinks. In my pocket, my hand wraps around my phone.

"Yes, please, Florence. Let her know I need her in the chapel," Mum finally says.

I let out a breath of relief. Hope's hand, which has been stuck on my face during this entire ordeal, falls limply to her side. I'm struck with a pang of regret—whatever chance I'd had at having my first kiss is gone. I can't put Hope in this position again.

*Ding dong!*

My heart drops as my phone's text message notification goes off. Who is texting me? Half of my contacts are within ten feet of me!

"Was that Aisling's phone?" Mum asks.

Before I can hear Florence's response—and what can she say really, aside from an outright lie?—Hope whispers, "Sorry, Your Highness!" and shoves me toward the back of the closet. My back hits the wall and the force of my weight causes the shelf above to rattle, the stacks of clean, folded towels tumbling down and over me. Hope rushes over and pulls more down, doing her best to cover me in the linens. As the door begins to open, my vision is blocked by a towel, and I can only hope that the rest of me is as hidden.

"What on Earth was that?" Mum's voice is much clearer now. My breath catches, praying she can't see me.

"Oh, Your Majesty!" Hope's voice is higher pitched than normal, and she sounds flustered. "I'm so sorry! I tripped and fell and—"

"It's fine," Florence cuts in. If she's surprised by the state of the closet, she doesn't sound it. "Just clean it up."

"Did a phone go off in there?" Mum asks.

"No, Your Majesty," Hope says. "I don't carry my phone with me when I'm working."

"I didn't hear anything," Florence adds. "I think you're overworking yourself, Your Majesty, especially with the wedding coming up."

The mention of my wedding makes me wince, burrowing further underneath the towels. If only I could hide in here forever.

"I think you're right, Florence," Mum agrees after a pause. "The stress is getting to me."

"I'll find Aisling and bring her to the chapel," Florence says. There's some slight shuffling, but no one else says a word. After a few moments, the towel is pulled off my face, and Hope's blue eyes bore into mine.

"That was way too close." She holds her hand out for me, and I take it, letting her pull me to my feet. I do my best to memorize the feel of her calluses against my palm, knowing this is probably the last time she'll touch me. Whatever Hope and I had, it's over now.

Florence stands in the doorway, silhouetted by the hall lights. "I agree. Why wouldn't you mute your phone?"

"I forgot!" I defend myself. I sigh and look at Hope. "I'm really sorry about this."

Hope's expression turns pained. "I am too. I don't think—I can't—"

"I know," I cut her off. "I wouldn't expect you to." Still, despite my words, there's a rock-like lump in my throat. Hope was so nice, and I was so close to getting my first kiss. But it feels like no matter how hard I try, I'm doomed to a life of hiding.

# CHAPTER TWO
# CHAVA

*Dear Chava Burke,*

*We regret to inform you that your application for the fall semester at Purdue University has been declined…*

I fold the letter closed, not wanting to read the rest of it, even though I have the whole thing memorized by now. It's probably not healthy, how many times I've stared at this letter, tracing my name or folding and refolding it until the creases threaten to tear.

"Staring at the letter isn't going to change their decision," my brother, Aaron, says, gaze trained on the paper-mâché volcano he's created for his camp science fair. I look over at him, taking in his curly hair, his round face, his light brown skin. He'd taken after our father, while I'd always looked more like Mama, my skin a slightly darker shade of brown than Aaron's. For most of my life, I'd never thought twice about it, but since Papa had died, I couldn't help but wish for some semblance of his features in my own. I'd stand in front of the mirror, scanning my eyes, my lips, my nose. Nothing ever came out.

Aaron peers inside the mouth of the volcano, then leans over and writes something in his notebook. He's still in the process of painting the stupid thing, newspaper spread over the table and pots of brown and red paint open. Irritation runs through me.

"Staring at your volcano won't show you the calculations," I shoot back.

"Actually, it will," Aaron says, not even bothering to spare me a glance. I frown. Since he turned thirteen, Aaron has had a holier-than-thou attitude, acting as if it's a chore to interact with me. Speaking of…

"It's your turn to do the dishes." I nod toward the sink, where dirty plates are doing their best impression of the Leaning Tower of Pisa.

"I'm busy," Aaron says. My frown gets deeper.

"It's your week. Don't be a brat."

"Chava," Dada, our grandfather, pipes up from his side of the table where he's doing his crossword. "Do the dishes for your brother. His science fair is this week."

"I've done the dishes the past two weeks because his science fair is this week," I argue. But I know it's no use.

When Papa died, things changed. I became invisible, second-thought.

"Just do it before you have to meet your mother." Dada looks pointedly at the note on our fridge—*Don't forget, Gracelynn's, 1 o'clock!* Once upon a time, she would've signed it with a *Love, Mama.* That time has come and gone.

"I'm supposed to meet Emilia in half an hour." The walk downtown is at least that, sometimes more if cars are assholes and won't let me cross the street.

"It won't kill you to be a little late in meeting your girlfriend," Dada says dismissively.

"*Ex*-girlfriend," I correct, my frustration building. Emilia and I had broken up two weeks ago. Even though it had been mostly mutual, I'd come home and stayed in bed for two days, crying into my pillow. Apparently, it hadn't made an impression.

"Just clean the dishes, Chava," Dada says, giving a sigh of long-suffering, as if I was the most difficult person in the world.

I bite my tongue and get up, going to the sink to start rinsing off the plates. I fight to keep the resentment from brewing, from angry tears forming. I don't want Dada or Aaron to see. I don't want to meet Emilia with red eyes and have her think I was crying over her.

"Crap!" Aaron shouts. I look over to see both pots of paint have tipped over, thick liquid spilling toward the edges of the table. Dada lifts his crossword without looking, completely unfazed. The rest of the table is covered in newspapers at least. Aaron can clean up his own mess.

My eyes catch on my letter from Purdue just as a mixture of red and brown overtake it.

"No!" I lunge for the letter, but it's too late. The paint has seeped through the thin paper, dyeing it a muddy brown color. I gingerly pick up the corner, but the weight of the liquid causes it to tear in half.

"What the hell, Aaron?"

"It's not my fault!"

"It literally is your fault!" I yell. "There is no one else who could be at fault here!"

"You're the one who left your letter on the table." Aaron shrugs.

"You little—"

"Chava," Dada interrupts, "it's just a piece of paper. They emailed it to you, too."

"And they rejected you," Aaron adds.

I crumple what remains of my letter into a ball and chuck it at his head. It hits him in the cheek with a wet *splat!*

"Eugh, Chava!" Aaron complains. He wipes at his face and glares at me.

"Chava!" Dada snaps. He's put his newspaper down, fixing me with a stare of equal parts frustration and disappointment. I open my mouth but close it almost immediately. I don't know what to say, and even if I did, it wouldn't make a difference. I hold his gaze for a moment, then two. He sighs and shakes his head. "Just do the dishes, then go meet up with your mother."

I clench my hands into fists, feeling the ooze of paint squeeze through my palm. Angry tears sting my eyes, but I fight them off and stalk back to the sink. I hold my hand under the water, letting it rinse off the dye. It washes down the drain, and a part of me wishes I could follow it.

# CHAPTER THREE
# AISLING

Florence and I make our way through the palace, reaching the heavy doors that lead to the sanctuary, a place where I've spent at least three hours every Sunday since I was born. Sometimes, it's suffocating in here, particularly when the preacher goes on and on about sinning and going against God. That was hard to wrestle with when I was younger—how I was starting to notice the daughters of the viscounts and barons who would attend the services all while the preacher would go on about how we should love thy gay neighbor but never, *ever* be like them.

Florence faces me and reaches out to straighten my jacket. She tugs it this way and that before brushing some invisible lint off my shoulders and nodding.

"Ready?" Florence asks. She hasn't mentioned the closet incident, and I doubt she will. My lady's maid has always been good about knowing when I want to talk about something; this is, decidedly, not one of those times.

I take a deep breath. "Yes."

Florence turns back to the doors and pushes them open, stepping aside for me to enter first. My eyes take a moment to adjust to the dark lighting, even with the sun shining in through the stained-glass window of the Virgin Mary. I look up at the front to see my mother talking to Father Peter, the priest who will marry me to my betrothed. My betrothed who, thankfully, and surprisingly, is absent.

My entrance draws my mother's attention.

"Aisling!" she cries, motioning for me to join her. "Come on up here, darling, we need to get started."

I walk down the middle aisle and try not to think about how I'll be walking down this very same aisle in a week, wearing a large white dress with a congregation of people staring at me. And that's not counting the millions of people who will be watching it live—apparently, my wedding needs to be both filmed *and* streamed, so it's readily available for everyone. Despite being a small European country—similar in size to Luxembourg, landlocked in-between a handful of countries—we're rather popular, due to my father being best friends with one of the princes of England. Lots of pictures and rumors from their young adulthood turned into keeping tabs on my father which turned into keeping tabs on me.

"Where is the duke?" I ask as I take the few steps up onto the dais to reach Mum.

She puts her hands on her hips and huffs. "His flight was delayed again, but he will most definitely be here tonight."

Brennan Lewis, the Duke of Belare—a province in Vyctorya—and my fiancé, was supposed to arrive yesterday afternoon, but the bad weather had delayed his trip so he wouldn't be here until today. I wondered how bad it must be storming for him to still not be here.

Maybe it isn't storms at all, but rather, his unwillingness to marry me. Briefly, I fantasize that he's actually hopped on a plane to fly to some faraway island and start a new life. We'd receive the news; my mother would be devastated, my father angry, but I would be completely and utterly free.

Of course, that would mean going against the crown, and no one has ever been brave enough to do that.

"Well," I say, "I suppose there's no reason for us to practice if the groom isn't here."

"Nonsense! I'd like for you to have some idea of what to expect on Saturday, and Father Peter would like to rehearse his part," Mum says.

I wonder how he isn't familiar with his part as a priest in a wedding, but then I remember the last wedding he'd officiated had been my parents', so he probably is a little rusty.

"And who's going to be the groom?" I ask.

"I will." My father has a way of taking up room, even with just his voice, which filters through the cracks and fills the empty spaces. I've always been envious of this ability of his, something that has always seemed to come naturally to him as the king. I turn around to see him strolling up the center aisle, an easy smile gracing his face.

"Shouldn't you be working?" Mum asks. Dad bounds up the steps to stand beside her and leans down to kiss her on the cheek.

"Work can wait," Dad says. "We've only got a few days left before we have to share her. I don't want to miss a moment of it."

A nasty feeling swirls and balls up in my stomach at the idea of the duke *sharing* me, but I push it down. It's my duty as the Crown Princess of Vyctorya to keep the bloodline going, to rule the country with a prince consort by my side.

"Shall we get started then?" Father Peter asks.

Dad nods and steps forward, grabbing my hands and moving me so that I face across from him. He winks, and I smile wryly. As Father Peter talks, I stare at my dad and take in the suntanned skin—lighter than my own and pinker—the brown hair streaked through with gray, the salt and pepper beard, and the total adoration shining through his blue eyes. To him, I can do no wrong.

I glance over at Florence. She smiles at me reassuringly, but I can't help the flashing thought of red hair and pale skin. Above me, I feel the Virgin Mary's stare on my back, her judgment clear.

The nasty feeling comes back, and this time I can't push it away.

After rehearsal wraps up, Florence walks me to my room, reminding me to be ready by six for dinner. I assure her I'll be properly primped, then beg off for a nap. I shut the door behind me with all the finality a soft *thud* can emit. Doors in the palace do not slam.

I groan and kick off the heels I've been wearing since seven this morning. I pick them up as I make my way to my bed—messes, no matter how small, make my brain itch. The comforter is pristine after a visit from the maids.

I run my hand over the downy fabric and wonder if Hope was one of the girls who made it up. My face heats, and I cover it with my hands. I lay back against the bed, letting my body sink into the feathers-stuffed mattress, and peek through my fingers at the floaty curtains that crisscross over the top of my bed.

What will happen to this room after next week? My mother has been so excited the past few months, readying what she calls the "Honeymoon Wing." She and my father had lived there for the years before my grandparents died, months before my birth. After that, they'd moved into the Royal Wing and raised me in this bedroom. Would this room not be used until I had a child? I shudder at the thought.

I sit up and lean over my nightstand, opening the topmost drawer that holds the Bible my father had given me. It had been his mother's. Flipping open the cover, I find the picture I'd stashed there of the duke—Brennan Lewis. White, pale with chiseled cheekbones and a Greek nose. Inky black hair curling past his ears, nearly to his chin. Ocean blue eyes. I stare at him, willing some sort of emotion to arise, for butterflies to erupt in my stomach, for a blush to stain my cheeks.

Nothing.

He's handsome enough, there's no denying that. Our children will most certainly be beautiful. If I try really hard, I can imagine little kids with a tan complexion and wildly curling hair, maybe a gap-toothed smile. But my stomach revolts at the thought. I take the picture and slip it into the drawer before slamming it shut.

I've done the same thing with that picture for months now, ever since my mother and father told me I was engaged to him. But nothing works. No matter how hard I try, I can't feel anything but loathing for this man who is going to take away my freedom, whether he means to or not.

Too keyed up to nap, I decide to change into a pair of gray athletic leggings and a shirt with a knit jacket and sneak down to the kitchens with the goal of drowning my sorrows in some chocolate chip cookies and milk, my sneakers only squeaking slightly on the marble floor.

When I walk into the kitchen, I'm surprised to find it fairly empty. The head chef, Leo, a middle-aged white man with streaks of gray in his blond hair, stands at a stainless-steel counter kneading dough, while some other cooks roam around, but there is maybe half the usual armada. I walk over to Leo and wait. After a few seconds, he looks up and notices me.

"Your Highness!" Leo lifts his hands and scratches his chin, leaving a streak of flour in his wake. "What are you doing down here?"

"I was hoping to steal some cookies," I say. "Do you have any?"

Leo smiles, wipes his hands on the towel at his hip, and motions for me to follow him. He leads me through the maze of counters and over to the cooling racks across from the ovens.

"Where is everyone?" I ask as he pulls out a tray of cookies and presents them to me. I grab one and take a bite, relishing the way the chocolate melts against my tongue.

"We got a delivery," he tells me. "Stuff for the wedding."

The cookie suddenly doesn't taste so great. I lick the crumbs off my lips and stare at the remainder of the dessert in my hand, trying to figure out how to get rid of it without Leo finding it weird.

Toward the back of the kitchen, the office door opens, and a cook walks out, swinging a ring of keys from his finger. My eyes track his journey across the kitchen. He stops at one of the stations to chat with a pastry chef who's kneading dough.

When I was younger, I used to come down to the kitchens almost every day to sneak sweets. Back then, the head chef had been an elderly man with a curly mustache and wisps of white hair on his otherwise bald head. I'd noticed that, at the same time on the same day, someone would leave the kitchens with a ring of keys. I'd asked the chef where they went, and he'd told me they sent someone to town every Sunday to gather fresh produce for the week.

After that, I'd paid more attention. I'd started to wear tennis shoes instead of my usual Mary Janes. I'd worn a jacket in the chillier months. And one day, I'd managed to sneak out after the cook. Unfortunately, my plan had been foiled, as I'd been too short to make it into the bed of the truck on my own.

When Florence had found out about my makeshift plan, she'd been livid. My parents had been even worse. I'd been banned from the kitchens for over a year, and by then, I'd given up on any hope of sneaking out.

Watching the cook flirting with the pastry chef now, I'm struck with the rebellious spirit my eight-year-old self had possessed. And I wonder if eighteen-year-old me has the same fire.

In all my life, I've rarely been allowed outside of the palace, and the handful of times I've been let out, it's always been covered behind security officers and bullet-proof glass. I've barely seen anything of Reneau, the capital of Vyctorya where we live, and I've never been further than the borders of Vyctorya itself.

Leo smiles and waves a hand, breaking me out of my thoughts. "Take as many as you want, Your Highness. I'm going to go back to my station."

I nod and grab another cookie from the tray with no intention of eating it. I turn to the rack as Leo moves away from me, tracking his reflection in the spotless steel of the large box next to the cooling racks. Everyone else in the kitchen seems focused on their tasks, so I slowly make my way toward the side door, keeping to the edge of the room.

The pastry chef flicks something at the cook, who laughs and backs away. He waves goodbye, makes his way to the door that leads outside, and exits. With a deep breath, I slip out several feet behind him, letting the door slam shut.

Heart pounding, I follow the cook. There's a delivery truck that people are unloading, but the cook heads in the opposite direction, toward a row of pickup trucks. I keep my head down and let my hair fall in front of my face, hoping no one pays too much attention to me. And why would they? It's not like I've got a tiara sparkling on my head.

The area outside of the kitchen is sparse, though there are a few boxes of herbs and spices that the kitchen grows. I duck behind one, watching the cook. My shoes are quiet on the cobblestones as I make for the space in between the two trucks on the end, crouching down so I can peek over the bed of the truck. The cook walks toward the fourth one, so I head around the back of the trucks and slink toward it. The vehicle beeps as he unlocks it. I look up to see if that caught anyone's attention, but they're all still focused on unloading boxes.

As he opens the door to slide in, I slowly pull down the hatch to the truck bed. It doesn't make a sound, so I scramble up into the bed and bring the hatch back into place at the same time he slams his own door shut. There's a pause, and I hold my breath. Then, the truck rumbles to life beneath me.

I lay flat on my back in the bed, heart pounding out of my chest. I can feel each individual *thump*. It thunders under my palms when I place my hands on my sternum.

What am I doing? What is my plan? I realize I have no plan—I just want to be a normal girl for once, even if that can never be true.

Is this really happening?

The truck stops. There are voices, loud and jovial.

"Where are you heading?" A guard at the gate, talking to the cook.

"Downtown," the cook says. "Picking up the usual. Benny's sick today."

"Yikes, anything serious?" the guard asks. "It can't be good to be down a cook the week before the wedding."

"Hopefully it's just a twenty-four-hour bug."

"Well." There's a slap against the roof. "You're good to go."

As the truck starts to move forward once more, I shrink as much as possible. The guard station isn't that high off the ground—I know from the few times I've been driven out in an armored car—so they shouldn't be able to look over the side of the truck and into the bed. I should be invisible. Nevertheless, I close my eyes.

Ten seconds. Thirty. A minute. Two.

I open my eyes. The sky above me is the same one that's inside the palace, but I can't help the smile that spreads across my face at the sight of it.

# CHAPTER FOUR
# CHAVA

I TIGHTEN MY GRIP ON THE BOX in my hands full of stuff from my failed relationship—sweaters I'd stolen, jewelry I'd been gifted, the CD I'd borrowed. Emilia stands across from me, holding a plastic sack with my own stuff. I set the box down on the table in the café that Emilia's family owns and slide it toward her. She hands me the bag.

"So," she says. Nothing else follows.

"So," I echo.

"We're still friends, right?" Emilia was the first person I met when I first moved to Vyctorya a year ago. She was beautiful, with her bright pink hair and her ebony skin. I hadn't expected that people in Vyctorya would be so beautiful; though to be perfectly honest, I hadn't expected much of anything from Vyctorya. I'd hated everything about the country my mother had grown up in and was now uprooting us to, purely out of principle. I'd been determined to keep myself isolated and ruminate in my misery.

But then I met Emilia.

We'd been friends, good friends, ever since, but a few months ago, we decided that we would give a relationship a try. It hadn't gone well.

"Of course, Em," I say. "I don't know what I'd do without you."

Tears gather in Emilia's eyes as she hugs herself. "Good. Me either."

Before I can overthink it, I pull her into a hug, my head coming to rest in the crook of her neck. She wraps her arms around me tightly and squeezes. Around us, the coffee shop is dead. It's never very busy on Sunday mornings; most people go to church in Vyctorya. Pulling back, I put my hands on her shoulders and smile.

"Hey," I say. "I still love you."

"I love you, too."

We say it, knowing that it's not the kind of love needed for a relationship. Maybe if I weren't so messed up, if my heart weren't already broken, I could make it work. But I can't, and Emilia deserves better.

"What are you doing the rest of the day?" Emilia asks, taking a step back to put more space between us. She wipes at her eyes.

I groan. "I have to go to Gracelynn's." The dress shop is surprisingly big, but it feels smaller with all the tulle and frills that are shoved into it. It makes me claustrophobic and small, which I hate. But my mother is insisting I get a dress for her fundraiser in a few days. She nearly had a conniption this morning when she'd learned that I still hadn't gone, and she threatened to choose one herself if I didn't have something to wear by tonight.

Emilia lets out a light laugh. "Oh no. Poor you."

"Shut up." I make a shoo-ing motion with my hands, and she laughs again. It makes my heart a little less heavy, that I can still make Emilia laugh. "You'll still be my date, right? To the fundraiser?"

"Of course," Emilia promises. She knows what the fundraiser means to me.

"Well, I have to get going," I say, glancing at the time on my phone. The sooner I get to the dress shop, the sooner I can leave.

"Here, let me walk you out."

I wrinkle my forehead. "You don't have to work?"

"I'm just going to run this box home real quick," she says, lifting the crate in her hands.

"And who's running the shop?" I ask teasingly. I look around at the empty café, though I do glance pointedly at where Kolby, a white guy with blue streaks through his blond hair who started last month, stands behind the counter.

"Dad." The *duh* is implied, but then she winces. "Wait, I didn't—"

I shake my head. "It's fine."

She looks at me a little sadly. "I hope you get the closure you need."

I say nothing, just loop the plastic bag around my wrist. Emilia adjusts the box in her grip, and we head out the door together. I think of all the times we've done this—both as friends, nudging into each other, and as a couple, holding hands, fingers intertwined. We don't hold hands now, and for the first time when we leave, we head in separate directions.

I walk down the sidewalk, stopping for a moment to look over my shoulder at Emilia's retreating form. My heart gives a twinge.

*I hope you get the closure you need.*

My phone dings, so I take it out of my pocket and type in my password. My home screen pops up, and I take in the picture of my father and me. We're in the hospital, but it was one of his good days, one of the days he could sit up and do a silly pose with me. I smile at the peace signs, at one of his arms slung across my shoulders. I can't believe it's been almost an entire year since he last hugged me.

I shake my head and go into my messages. Mama's wondering where I'm at. I sigh as I type out an *on my way* before putting my phone away.

As I walk to Gracelynn's, Emilia's words ring through my head, her voice echoing throughout my skull. They make my skin itch, but they are also admittedly nicer than the ones she'd said to me during the explosive fight that was our breakup two weeks ago.

*You can't give me your heart if it's still broken over your father.* She'd thrown them like knives, and they'd hit their mark. But the pain of her words had been sharp; they'd sliced through me cleanly. The pain of my father's death was dull, and it hacked through me every day.

I try to shake it off as Gracelynn's Dress Shop comes into view and with it, my mother. She stands in the window, kneeling in front of a mannequin and messing with the hem of its dress, a fabric tape measure strung around her neck. She's wearing a white button-up shirt that stands out against her brown skin and black slacks, her ebony hair pulled up in a bun. She straightens up, dusting off her knees, and when she sees me, she motions for me to come inside.

I walk through the door, the bell above it jingling a welcome. The sound makes me wince every time, and that's saying a lot given how often I'm here. The owner, Gracelynn herself, is my godmother, and she swiftly brought my mom along as her assistant when we moved.

Before Mama and Papa met, she'd wanted to be a designer. She and Gracelynn had had a plan of opening a shop in Vyctorya, but then Mama met Papa and moved to America, and Gracelynn opened her shop anyway.

Mama pounces immediately, grabbing my arm and dragging me through the store to the back. We reach the dressing rooms, and she shoves me in unceremoniously. I turn around to catch a glimpse of her face—pinched, a permanent pucker in between her eyebrows, her lips a thin line nearly forming a frown—before the curtain is pulled across the steel bar, and she disappears from my sight.

"I've picked out some dresses for you," she says, her voice floating through the velvet fabric of the curtain. "They're hanging on the rack." I turn to see five dresses, ranging in color from a dull gray to a sparkling silver. They're all floor-length, but they vary in the neckline, the sleeve-length, the waist. I sigh and pull off the first one, the most lackluster gray made out of some sort of filmy material with cap sleeves and an empire waist.

"We want gray," Mama continues as I slip out of my clothes and into the dress, "for brain cancer awareness." It's a little tight when I try to zip it up, so I pull back the curtain and present the back to my mother. She tugs the zipper up little by little until it's resting at the base of my neck.

I turn around, arms spread as wide as I can—which isn't far at all—to let her look at the way the bodice hugs my chest. She hums and reaches out to pick and pull at places on the dress. She frowns and takes a step back.

"Spin," she orders. I obey.

"Since this is a formal event, I think we should keep the long skirt. But the sleeves…" she trails off, ghosting a hand down my arm. I can't remember the last time my mother patted my arm or hugged me or kissed my cheek. She's been keeping her distance—though whether it's purposeful or accidental, I don't know. The way she's been avoiding everything else in life, I have a feeling it's purposeful.

"Sleeveless." She nods to herself. "It will show off your arms."

I glance at my arms. I don't notice anything about them that warrants showing off.

"Next dress," she says, shooing me back into the dressing room. I grab the curtain before she can pull it closed.

"Mama," I begin, "I don't—It's just—I can't—"

"What?" Mama asks, impatient. She crosses her arms over her chest and taps her finger against her arm.

*I don't want to go to the fundraiser.*

*It's just so hard pretending I'm fine.*

*I can't do this.*

*Why can't you see that I can't do this?*

"Nothing. Nevermind," I say and let her slide the curtain closed.

# CHAPTER FIVE
# AISLING

It doesn't take long to get downtown. The cook pulls into a brick alley and stops the truck. He gets out, slamming the door shut behind him. I listen to his footsteps—a door opens, then closes.

I peek over the side of the truck, checking to see if the coast is clear. The cook is nowhere to be found, so I climb over the back of the truck and jump down onto the ground, the balls of my feet stinging from the sudden impact. When my tennis shoes touch the asphalt, my stomach rolls. I can't tell whether it's out of fear or elation. Maybe a mix of both.

The alley is the most disgusting place I've ever been in. The red brick is pretty well taken care of, but there are splatters of mysterious substances all over it. Somewhere, there's water dripping—a leak? Several trash cans decorate the alley as well, some of their lids only part way on so that the smell of garbage permeates the small space. I gag a little as I pass by one.

I make my way to the end of the alley, pulling my hood up over my hair so that it hopefully hides my face a little better. My foot catches at one point, and I look down to see that I've stepped in something sticky and pink. Gum? I've never had gum before; Mum was convinced it was a one-way ticket to a cavity. I wrinkle my nose as I try to scrape the candy off the bottom of my shoe. It smears even more, so I give up and keep an eye on the ground as I walk.

At the junction where the alley meets the street, I hesitate, setting my hand on the brick beside me. The roughness of the material underneath my fingertips grounds me, makes me think.

I could turn back—climb back into the truck, keep hidden until we're back at the palace, and sneak back up to my room without anyone ever being the wiser. Or I could take a chance.

I close my eyes, take a breath, and step out onto the street.

Nothing happens.

I open my eyes and look around. The street I'm standing on is fairly empty. There are several cars parked along the sidewalk, but their owners are nowhere to be found. On the opposite side, there's a group of three teenagers who giggle their way into a shop. I look up at the sign to see where they went: *Espresso Yourself.* It must be a coffee shop.

Before I can talk myself out of it, I head across the street toward the shop. A car comes out of nowhere and stops just short of me, honking its horn in annoyance. I raise a hand in apology and hurry the rest of the way to the sidewalk.

The exterior of the coffee shop is made out of windows and a rich, dark wood. The door is glass, but it's outlined in gold metal. I grab the golden handle and pull the door open. There are a few musical notes as I step inside, the doorbell announcing my presence.

Round tables, each with four seats, are spaced out around the shop. At the back, there is a long counter made from the same wood that makes up the exterior. Above it, there is a wooden light fixture with Edison bulbs that flood the station in a warm, yellow glow. A coffee machine with a screen sits on one end of the counter while a cash register sits on the other, a glass display of pastries in the middle.

"Welcome! I'll be with you in just a moment!" The voice, a Black girl with her neon pink box braids pulled back from her face, stands next to the coffee machine, utterly focused on her task. I walk closer and stand by the register, looking around. The menu is hung up above my head, and as my eyes scan it—coffees, teas, pastries—I remember that I don't have any money.

I start to take a step back when the girl comes over, smiling brightly. From this close, I can see the golden undertones of her skin, the warmth that exudes from her face. She reminds me of the sun. She's beautiful, with a heart-shaped face and mesmerizing brown eyes and a round nose. Her eyes light up as she takes my face in, and my breath catches—is this what they talk about in books, what happens in movies, when two people meet and it's love at first sight?

Do I even know what love is? Looking at her face, I feel like I could.

"Chava," the girl says, "I didn't think I'd see you here."

My heart deflates, but then confusion filters through the disappointment. Who's Chava, and why does this girl think I'm them?

"Uh…" My eyes catch on her nametag—Emilia.

"Are you okay? Is something wrong?" Emilia asks, worry coloring her tone. I take a stumbling step back, and she leans forward over the counter.

"No, nothing's wrong!" My voice goes up a pitch from nervousness, and I cough. "I just, um, I think you have me confused with someone else."

Emilia frowns. "What are you talking about?"

The group of teenagers I saw earlier stand a few feet away at the end of the counter, holding their drinks and giggling. When I lock eyes with one of the girls, the giggling gets louder.

"Are you the princess?" the girl asks.

My breath catches.

"Right," Emilia scoffs, shooting me an amused look. "Like the crown princess of Vyctorya would come to a coffee shop in the middle of town."

I let out a high-pitched laugh, trying to brush it off like Emilia. Everyone stares at me.

This is too much. I feel like I'm underwater, slogging through freestyle strokes. I was never a very strong swimmer.

I turn and bolt out the door.

"Chava!" Emilia calls. I ignore her and fling the door open, stepping outside. I look left, right, checking to see if anyone is coming. There's someone far down on the right sidewalk, so I turn left and head down the sidewalk, fast walking but not running.

I keep my head down, eyes on my feet as I make my way down the street. It's just as empty. It makes me nervous.

Suddenly, bells begin ringing. They overlap each other, so much so that it becomes almost painful to listen to. It nearly knocks me to my knees when I realize that, in a week, those bells will be ringing because of my marriage. I pause on the sidewalk and glance around, looking for a fairly empty shop I might hide out in to get my bearings. To my left, there is a large glass window that displays several glitzy dresses. I hesitate, then pull the door open.

There's a little jingling above me, but it ends as soon as the door closes behind me. The sound of the church bells is muffled in here, and I surge deeper, intent on getting lost in the racks. Maybe it'll cushion the sound entirely.

I glance around the shop, taking in the wide variety of dresses on display. One side is almost entirely wedding dresses, while formal dresses mirror them on the opposite wall. There's a cream upholstered couch in the middle of the shop sandwiched between two blue chairs styled in the same fashion. In front of it, there is a little pedestal where I imagine future brides stand to try on different dresses, eager to find "the one."

I didn't get to choose my wedding dress. My mother had an idea and commissioned it with that in mind alone. I've tried it on a couple of times, but it's always been a blur. I remember lace and billowing skirts, but other than that, there's nothing. I've blocked it out in the hopes that I won't have to wear it.

I walk further toward the back of the shop where the dressing rooms are. They're quaint, with pastel floral-patterned curtains acting as the doors.

"Mama!" A girl steps out of the dressing room, her head tilted down to face the floor. Her short, dark brown hair falls in front of her face, obscuring it. "This one isn't so bad."

She looks up. Her amber eyes meet mine. My mouth drops open. So does hers. It's like looking in a mirror.

This girl has my face.

# CHAPTER SIX
# CHAVA

For a second, I wonder if I'm still asleep and having one of the weirdest, most depressing dreams ever. Was this morning in the kitchen real? Did I meet up with Emilia? I pinch the soft skin at my wrist and wince. I'm not dreaming. The girl across from me is real, and it's like looking in a mirror.

Her hair is longer than mine and a few shades darker, black to my dark brown. Her tan skin is smooth and clear where I have freckles sprinkled across my nose and cheeks, and her eyes are more golden than amber, a shade or two lighter than my own. She holds herself almost painfully straight, her chin tilted up as if she was born to be someone important. She's both the complete opposite of me and my twin at the same time.

We have the same round eyes, the same round nose, the same point to our chins. It's uncanny.

"Holy shit," I breathe. I take a step forward, reaching out a hand carefully, like if I touch her, she'll disappear. Like a mirage. The girl cocks her head and opens her mouth to say something when there's a slam from somewhere in the shop.

The girl whips back to face me. "Hide me!" she whispers urgently. My eyes widen.

"What?"

"Please," she begs, "no one can see me."

I take a split second to deliberate before pulling her into the dressing room with me and pulling the curtain halfway closed, so she's just barely out of sight.

Mama comes around the corner and puts her hands on her hips.

"What did you say, Chava?" she asks.

"I think this dress is the one," I say, hyper aware of the fact that I'm hiding a random girl who looks like me from my mother.

Mama hums and steps forward. I step back. She frowns.

"What are you doing?" she asks.

"I just really like this one," I lie. It's not terrible, as far as dresses go—a shiny silver fabric with spaghetti straps and a flowy skirt. It's the least restrictive thing I've tried on today, and I feel like I can survive the fundraiser in it. "I don't want you to find anything wrong with it."

Mama crosses her arms and surveys me, eyes roaming up and down and up again. After a moment, she shrugs. "I agree. I think it's the one."

My eyebrows nearly fly off my face. "You do?"

Mama nods. "Take it off, so we can go ring it up."

I stand there for a moment and bite my lip.

Mama arches an eyebrow. "What?"

"Nothing," I say, voice a pitch higher than it should be. I step back into the dressing room and drag the curtain across the metal rod, the rings *ting*ing across. I turn around to look at the girl. She's staring at me, looking stricken, hands in her hair.

"What am I going to do?" she whispers, her voice laced with panic.

"Face the wall," I tell her. I need to change, and while this girl may be my long-lost twin or something, she doesn't need to see *every* part of me. She spins so that she's facing the wall, and I turn so that my back is to her, too. I unzip the dress and slide the straps off my shoulders, letting the fabric pool at my feet.

"Make sure you hang the dress up!" Mama orders from outside. "I don't want it getting wrinkled!"

I groan. "Yes, Mama."

The bell above the door rings, and Mama calls out a welcome. I quickly get dressed, throw my purse across my shoulder, and pick the dress up off the floor before putting it on a hanger and hanging it on the wall. I peer out through the curtain to see that Mama has stepped away to help the customer. I glance back at the girl and motion for her to follow me.

We slink through the small dressing area, and I lead the girl toward the back of the shop. The door to the back, the place where Gracelynn makes her dresses and plans her sketches, is unlocked—that must have been where Mama went when I ran into my mystery twin—so I ease it open and push the girl ahead of me. It clicks softly shut behind us. I breathe a sigh of relief.

"There's a door that leads to the alley back here. We can use that to sneak out," I tell the girl, leading the way. "By the way, why are we sneaking out?" I glance over my shoulder at the girl, and she runs her tongue over her bottom lip.

"I can explain everything," she tells me. We make it to the door. I open it and hop down the two steps. She follows down daintily, stepping with the ball of her foot before ending with the heel.

"How about you start by telling me your name?" I ask.

The girl looks at me hesitantly. "It's… Aisling."

"Like the princess?" I scoff.

She says nothing.

The realization is a punch to the gut. "Holy shit—like the *princess?*"

When I first moved to Vyctorya, people would often tell me that I resembled the crown princess of Vyctorya. Emilia had teased me about it all the time. Sometimes, when I'd ask her to do something—get me a drink, help me with Calculus—she'd smirk and say, *Yes, Your Highness.* I would scoff, so one day, she finally showed me a picture of the princess.

It was from a couple of years ago, on her sixteenth birthday, and while there was a passing resemblance, I didn't put much stock in it. She was beautiful and regal and above it all. It was probably photoshopped a little too— who was to say that her nose was that straight?

But looking at the girl in question, I wished I'd looked a little closer at the picture. Maybe I wouldn't have been so blindsided.

The girl—Aisling—the *princess*—winces and holds a finger to her lips. I guess I'd said that louder than I thought. She looks around warily, but we're the only ones in this alley. It's fairly narrow, and Gracelynn's is the only shop that leads out to it. Beside me, there are several trash cans that are overflowing with scraps of fabric and bits of thread.

"I snuck out," the princess tells me. She shrugs helplessly. "I don't know what I'm doing."

My phone rings before I can give a response. I pull it out of my pocket—my mother. I groan.

"Hang on a second," I tell the princess. I answer the call.

"Where did you go?" Mama demands.

"I wasn't feeling well," I lie.

"What do you mean? Like a cold? Nauseous?"

"A cold," I say. "Kind of dizzy."

"So, where did you go?" Mama asks again.

"I'm headed home to lay down."

"While you're dizzy? Chava." Mama sighs a breath out of her nose. "Call me when you get home, so I know you didn't pass out on the side of the street."

"Yes, Mama," I say and hang up the phone, shoving it back into my pocket. I turn back to the princess. Her eyes dart everywhere, from my face to the alley ground up to the cloudy sky above.

"What now?" I ask. It's probably more attitude than I should be giving the princess, but I'm confused and still upset from earlier, and I honestly just want to go home and curl up in my bed.

The princess starts a little at my voice and focuses on my face, as if she'd been lost in thought. "Have you ever wanted to be a different person?"

I blink. "What kind of question is that?"

"Come on," the princess says. "You can't tell me you have the perfect life."

"Of course I don't!" I snap.

"Exactly!" She springs forward, grabbing me by the shoulders. I'm too shocked to stop her. "What if I told you that you *could* be a different person? Just for a week?"

The pieces are slowly coming together. Does she mean…

"You're crazy," I say. "Are you trying to say you want to switch places with *me*? You don't even know me!"

"But you know me!" the princess says. "Anyone would kill to be a princess!"

"No, no, no." I shake my head. "This is insane—you're saying insane things! Do you even hear yourself?"

"Please," the princess says, her voice soft, her fingers squeezing my shoulders. "Do you ever… do you ever just wish you could disappear?"

"Yeah." I frown. "Do you?"

The princess's eyes water, but they stay locked on mine. "All the time," she whispers. On my shoulders, her hands shake.

I swallow, then let out a breath. Reaching up, I pull her hands off me.

"This is a terrible idea," I say as I yank my phone out of my pocket.

"What are you doing?" Her eyes are wide.

"Typing notes," I tell her.

"Why?"

"How are you going to pretend to be me if you don't know anything about me?" I ask.

The princess's eyes widen. "Really?"

"Here." I hand the princess my phone and purse. "Where's yours?"

"At the palace," the princess says.

"Great, and how am I supposed to get back in there?" I ask.

"I, uh, don't know." She bites her lip. She looks around as if the dirty alleyway will give her an answer. Then, she squeaks and ducks behind the trash cans.

"Aisling!" The voice is hushed, irritated, and commanding. I look behind me at the end of the alley that leads to a back street. There's a black car idling there, and a tall woman striding toward us, anger written across her beautiful features. She wears a bright blue pantsuit that stands out against her brown skin, and her glossy black hair is pulled back in a high ponytail. When she gets closer, I see that she has a dark beauty mark above her lip.

She marches up to me and grabs my arm. "What the hell were you thinking?"

"Um. Ow." I wince as her nails, long and glossy and pointed, dig into the fleshy part of my upper arm.

"I don't want to hear it," the woman snaps. She begins to drag me back down the alley toward the car. I glance at the trash cans once more, but I can't see the princess. I take a deep breath and let it out. I guess I'm really doing this— not like the princess has given me much of a choice.

I'm shoved in the back of the car, and the woman slides in behind me.

"Drive," she orders the driver, whipping out her phone. Typing away, she speaks toward me once more: "I cannot believe you pulled this stunt. I am not letting you out of my sight until the wedding, do you understand?"

"Uh… yes?" I say.

The woman looks up at me. Her eyes bulge. "What the hell happened to your hair?"

# CHAPTER SEVEN
## AISLING

I WAIT UNTIL I HEAR THE CAR drive away. Once I'm sure the coast is clear, I stand up from behind the trash cans.

I can't believe that worked. I look down at the girl's phone—Chava. I click the side button to turn it on and am thankful when it opens. My face works to unlock her phone as well. The notes app is open. At the top is an address—113 Cherry Tree Lane. That must be where she lives. Scrolling down, I see some she's typed some other things:

*Mama—Melissa Burke*

*Brother—Aaron Burke, 13*

*Dada—Gian Laghari*

*Emilia Taylor*

My eyes zero in on the name Emilia. That was the girl from the coffee shop's name, the one who'd called me

Chava. I wonder who she is to my mysterious doppelgänger.

I shake my head to clear my thoughts. That's not important right now. First, I need to figure out how to get to Chava's house. I can't just stand out on the streets of Reneau. Despite the fact that Chava clearly looks like me and has gone unnoticed, I don't trust someone not to recognize me.

Putting in the address in the Maps app, I follow the directions. It takes me through the streets, passing squat, brick buildings, all attached to one another. Eventually, the buildings thin out and residential houses begin to pop up. I stare at it all, taking every inch in. I've never been to this part of Reneau. When I have been allowed out of the palace, which was few and far between, we only went to certain places—the park to unveil a statue, the children's hospital to read to the kids. I've never gotten to see the city.

It's a long walk. The dress shop was in the middle of the town, and Chava apparently lives on the outskirts. For a moment, I wonder if I should try to order one of those car rides I've seen on T.V., but I quickly dismiss the idea.

Eventually, I turn into a small neighborhood and stop in front of a quaint little two-story house, painted white with blue shutters. The phone tells me I've arrived. I walk up the manicured lawn, pausing to admire the little garden of flowers beside the front door. I take a deep breath, looking up at the house before me. I open the door—or try to. It's locked. Right.

I pull out Chava's purse—more of a tote bag, really, though it does have a lot of pockets. I find a keychain and pull it out, trying multiple keys in the lock until I get the right one. Slowly, I open the front door and step inside.

"Hello?" I call out. No answer. To my immediate left is a set of stairs, and I take them up to the second floor, which consists of a hallway with doors on either side. I go to the closest one and open it up. The room is orange with posters on the walls and beads hanging down over the bed, which is in the middle of the wall, covered in a bright blue comforter. There are some bean bags on the floor, and the desk off to the side is messy with a laptop in the corner. I take a step inside and notice a cork board beside the door filled with pictures of Chava and other people. So, this is her room.

I turn around in a circle, taking in the space I'll be staying in for the next few days. It's nice, smaller than my room, but that was to be expected. The lava lamp I see on the bedside table only cements the 70s vibe; all she needs is a record player and I'd be transported in time.

I turn back to the pictures, examining them. Most of them are of Chava with an older white man. Sometimes, a boy is in them, too—her brother, Aaron, I assume. There's also a wedding photo, showcasing two people who must be her parents, the same man standing in a tuxedo, grinning next to a beautiful bride in a gorgeous gown. My eyes skim the rest of the pictures, pausing on the familiar face of Emilia. She and Chava are dressed formally, arms around each other, standing in front of a balloon arch. They're beaming, Emilia's head resting on Chava's shoulder. I smile, then I frown, looking closer at Chava.

Her hair is short. Mine is long.

I bite my lip, trying to remember how long Chava's hair was earlier today. A little past her chin? I take in a deep breath, then let it out.

There's only one thing to do.

Going to the desk, I rummage around in the drawers. I find a pair of scissors easily enough, then turn to the mirror hanging beside the door. I gather my long, dark hair in a ponytail and try to guess about where to cut. Bit by bit, I chop away at my hair, hoping it doesn't look too awful. No one will notice if it's an inch or two off, right?

When I'm done, I throw my hair away in the trash can by Chava's bed. I sit down and put my head in my hands. I can't believe I just did that. Florence is going to have a field day when I get back.

I sit up straighter and shake my head. It will be fine. I've never been the rebellious type; what's a major haircut days before my wedding?

A door downstairs slams shut.

"Chava? Are you home?" a voice calls out.

My hands grip my knees tightly. This is it, the moment of truth.

I get up and go downstairs.

# CHAPTER EIGHT
# CHAVA

THE WOMAN TAKES ME UP TO the princess's room through a backway, passing a few maids. One, a redhead with milk-white skin, pauses, opening her mouth as if to say something. The woman stops so quickly, I run into her back. She shoots me a look, but I just look down at my feet. I've been playing subservient since she yelled at me about my hair.

"Yes, Hope?" she says impatiently.

"I, uh, wanted to apologize for earlier, Lady Florence," the girl says. She peers around the woman—Florence, apparently—and makes eye contact with me, something meaningful swimming in her eyes. I keep my face neutral, and hers falls.

"Accidents happen," Florence says stiffly. "Just don't let it happen again."

Hope swallows and nods before continuing on her way. Florence starts walking once more, and I hurry to keep up. A few more turns, and Florence flings open a set of double doors, practically shoving me inside.

I pause, taking in my luxurious surroundings. The princess's bedroom—which is what this must be—is bigger than my living room. It's mostly white with pink accents here and there: the comforter on the king-sized canopy bed, the two couches set up on the other side of the room as if someone might stop by for tea, the gigantic rug that covers half of the marble floor. There's even a bay window with a pink cushion and white, lacy curtains. I feel like I just stepped into… well, a princess's room.

"The duke has arrived," Florence announces. I turn to face her. "That's what I was coming to tell you when I realized you were missing."

"Oh." I wrack my brain for any information about a *duke*. Vaguely, I recall hearing something about the princess marrying a duke on the news when Dada was watching. Is that duke *this* duke? It has to be. "Okay."

Florence stares at me as if waiting for some reaction. I don't know which one to give her—is the princess angry about her engagement? Happy? I search Florence's face for some sort of hint and come up empty.

"You'll have dinner with him tonight, along with your mother and father," Florence continues. At that, my heart nearly stops. Dinner with the *king and queen?* But I can't panic in front of her. Instead, I nod.

"I… suppose I should get dressed?" My statement comes out as more of a question. Florence cocks her head but nods.

"Yes," she says. "There's an outfit laid out for you in your closet."

"Right." The closet. Where is the closet? I turn to walk further into the room, looking for a door to a closet. There's a set of double doors, and I push them open, thanking my luck when I'm greeted by a large room with clothes spanning the perimeter. There's a large ottoman—pink, of course—in the middle of the room with a dress lying on it.

The dress is pink, like a strawberry milkshake, and just as frothy. Layers of skirts swing around my knees as I pull it on, while the bodice hugs tight to my chest with spaghetti straps to hold it up. I look at myself in the mirror and frown, but I go back out to meet Florence anyways.

"I don't know what we're going to do about your hair," Florence tells me, "but there's nothing to be done tonight. Finish getting ready."

I open my mouth to tell her I *am* ready—as ready as I can be to meet the king and queen of a nation—when she motions toward the vanity. I walk over to it and find a wide variety of makeup. I settle on a layer of mascara and lip gloss and pick up a brush to run through my short hair. Florence watches me the whole time; I try my best to hide how my hand shakes.

"Are you ready?" she asks.

*No.* "Yes."

Florence turns on her heel and walks out of the room. I hurry to follow her, trying my best not to trip in the heels I've put on. Once again, Florence leads me through the palace, but this time, it's the main area. We pass through what I assume to be the residential area, the walls filled with pictures of the current royal family. There are marble columns that line the hall, and the long rug that runs along the floor is plush under my feet. When we get to the part of the palace where more people see, it becomes even fancier, decked out in garish reds and golds with fleur-de-lis everywhere. There are ropes sectioning off areas like grand pianos and old antique desks. There are also paintings, most larger than my couch, and sculptures everywhere. It's like a museum.

"I've gotten some reports from the maids." Florence's tone is hushed as we make our way to the marble staircase and start our descent. "From their account, he's kind. He was very thankful when Alfonse took his suitcases up to the room where he'll be staying. He made a point to introduce himself to the maid who is in charge of cleaning the room." She pauses, waiting for a response.

"That's... good."

"Perhaps," Florence begins, "when you've gotten to know each other better, you could tell him." She looks at me expectantly. *Tell him what?* I want to ask, but I know that would be about the most stupid thing I could do. Instead, I give her a weak smile.

"Maybe," I agree.

Eventually, we arrive at a set of open double doors that Florence marches through with a confidence I could never hope to possess. She introduces me and pushes me forward. I'm blinded by the chandelier sparkling above; I blink. There's a gasp.

"Aisling!" A woman at the end of the table stands up, a hand at her mouth. "What did you do to your hair?"

"A little teenage rebellion," Florence says smoothly. "We'll get it fixed first thing tomorrow morning, Your Majesty. I've already called Luka."

My hand goes up to my hair a little self-consciously. The queen looks like she wants to cry.

"I don't think it looks so bad, Krisha," a middle-aged man at the head of the table says. The King. I gulp. He motions for me to come to the table, gesturing toward an empty seat next to the last person in the room. He turns to look at me, standing up, and our eyes meet—amber on blue. My stomach drops. He's the most handsome man I've ever seen, his black hair such a contrast against his white skin that it takes my breath away. He bows deeply.

"It's a pleasure to make your acquaintance, Your Highness," he says, looking up at me from under his eyelashes. He straightens up. "Oh, uh, I'm Brennan Lewis, Duke of Belare."

"Yes," I say when no one else says anything, hoping my voice isn't as shaky as I feel. "It's nice to meet you too."

Florence nudges me in the back, and I realize I've been staring. I quickly take my seat, keeping my gaze firmly fixed to the table. A clap sounds through the room and suddenly there are several people all around us, all with bowls in hand. A lady sets one down in front of me: a broth of some sort with carrots and celery and other things floating in the liquid.

"Well, no need to hold back," the king says, the tone of his voice like an announcement. "Let's eat! I'm starving!" I do as I'm told, remaining quiet and only speaking when spoken to. Mostly, the king and queen ask the duke questions about himself, which he answers. Sometimes, he directs things to me, but for the most part, I'm able to sit back and do my best to not make a fool of myself.

Finally, after two hours and several courses, the king pushes back from the table and stands up, the queen following. The duke immediately stands up as well, and I scramble to do the same.

"Well, I apologize for leaving so soon, but I'm afraid I do have some work I need to finish up," the king says. He motions to someone off to the side, and a butler appears. "Alfonse will show you to your room, Your Grace." The duke bows to the king and queen before turning to me.

"I look forward to getting to know you, Your Highness," he says. He holds his hand out, and, mesmerized, I give my own to him. He presses a soft kiss to the back of my hand, and I think I nearly black out. His lips are warm against my skin and smooth like silk. He lets go and leaves the room. I blink, dazed. Then, I glance around the room, looking for Florence, only to realize she's not here. I panic—how the hell am I supposed to find my way back to the princess's room?

The queen descends upon me before I can worry too much. She loops her arm through mine and begins leading me through the palace, back up the staircase I'd gone down earlier.

"So…" she says, dragging out the word. I say nothing. "What did you think of him?"

"He seems… nice," I finally answer. That does not satisfy the queen.

"Come on," she says. "When he kissed your hand, *I* nearly swooned."

I stifle a laugh, but a bit of a giggle comes out anyway. The queen gives me a knowing smile and squeezes my arm tighter. I'm struck with the memory of doing the same thing with my own mother, back before Papa died. How we'd sit on my bed and giggle with each other, eating candy and popcorn, talking about my crushes or gossiping about the people at school or her work. Mama had been my best friend, and when I lost Papa, I lost her, too.

"I know this isn't ideal, but I really think there could be something between you two someday," the queen continues.

"Maybe," I say. The queen simply smiles knowingly and continues walking. We reach the princess's bedroom, and she stops me, turning me to face her. She tilts my head down so she can kiss the top of it, then hugs me—hard. "I love you."

There is a lump in my throat the size of a rock. I work to swallow it down so I can respond.

"I—I love you, too," I tell her. She pulls back and smiles at me one last time before wishing me a goodnight and turning to leave. I open the door to the princess's room, shutting it behind me and leaning back against it. I fight the urge to cry, fight the urge to think about the last time my mother told me she loved me. I take a deep breath and stand up straight, heading for the closet. I just want to get out of this dress and into something comfortable. That huge bed, soft and inviting, is calling my name.

I make it two steps when I realize Florence is sitting on one of the couches. She's got a tea set in front of her and is sipping from her own cup. She sets it down on the table, then turns to face me, folding her hands primly in her lap.

"You're not Aisling."

# CHAPTER NINE
# AISLING

Everyone is in the kitchen when I make it downstairs. An old man sits at the table, legs folded while filling out a newspaper—Gian, I presume—while a woman stands at the sink, washing her hands. Melissa. She looks at me over her shoulder, and I'm both surprised and not to see that she barely resembles my mother at all. They both have brown skin and dark eyes, but that's pretty much where the similarities end. She frowns at me, turning back to the sink. A boy with slightly lighter skin and dark, curly hair also sits at the table, writing in a notebook and sitting next to a papier-maché volcano on the table. This must be Aaron.

"How was your day, Chava?" Gian asks, adjusting his glasses on his nose. "Anything exciting happen?"

It's such a strange way to phrase the question that for a moment, I worry he's figured it out already. But how could he?

"Uh, no, nothing special," I say.

"When did you get home?" he prods. His eyes have a knowing look that makes me uncomfortable. *Could* he know?

"About half an hour ago," I tell him.

Melissa turns to look at me, wiping her hands on her jeans. Her brow furrows. "Is there—what's wrong with your voice?" she asks. I'm grateful for the change in conversation.

"Oh, uh, I think I'm getting a cold."

Melissa sighs. "You're still saying that?"

I look around, searching for an answer I can't find.

"It's just some coughing, making me hoarse, I guess," I say.

"You're not getting out of the fundraiser," she announces, pointing at me with her finger. Fundraiser? What fundraiser?

For a second, I worry about what I've gotten myself into.

"I'm not trying to," I say. Melissa stares at me for a moment, as if she doesn't believe me.

"Well, we're having spaghetti for dinner," she says, motioning to the pot on the stove. Steam rises from it. "It should be ready in about twenty minutes."

I nod, wondering what I'm supposed to do for the next twenty minutes. Go back upstairs? Stand around awkwardly?

Gian saves me.

"Why don't you come help me with this crossword puzzle?" he offers, motioning to the seat beside him, across from Aaron. I go over to him and sit down, looking at the puzzle. He's got about half of it done, and I really don't know what help he needs, but it's better than standing around doing nothing.

We spend the next twenty minutes working on the puzzle. Every once in a while, I glance up to see Aaron giving me a strange look, but he always looks away before I can figure out why he's staring at me. By the time Melissa pulls out a pan of garlic bread, we've finished the puzzle, and I've found I've actually enjoyed bantering with Gian.

"Chava, will you set the table?" Melissa asks.

"Uh, sure," I say. Etiquette lessons made sure that I knew what a properly set table looked like, even though it was mainly to ensure I knew which fork was for salad and which was for dessert.

I walk to the nearest cabinet and open it—pots and pans. I glance over my shoulder to make sure Melissa is not paying attention to me as I quietly shut the door and move onto the next one. Luckily, this one is filled with plates and bowls. I grab four plates and set them on the counter. It takes me three tries to find the drawer with the silverware, but when I do, I pick up four forks and four spoons. I gather everything up in my arms and head to the table on the opposite side of the kitchen.

It's a round, wooden table, with four chairs around it. It sits beside a sliding glass door which leads out to a fenced-in backyard. I begin to set the places, doing my best to work around the volcano. I accidentally bump it, though, when I set down Aaron's plate.

"Hey, watch it!" he grumbles.

"Oh, sorry," I say.

He quirks an eyebrow. "No sassy reply?"

I open my mouth and shut it. Should I give a sassy reply?

"Aaron, don't antagonize your sister," Gian says. "Chava, would you mind getting the drinks? Since you're already up? I'll take water."

Another task? I keep my mouth closed and squeak out an affirmative response.

"What do you want to drink?" I ask Aaron cheerfully, hoping to throw him off.

The kid doesn't blink. "Water."

That seems strange for a thirteen year old to ask for—wouldn't he go for soda, or at least juice?—but I shrug it off. I go over to the cabinets and choose the one beside the cabinet that holds the plates, praying it's the right one. It is. Quickly, I grab four glasses and set them on the counter.

"Mama, what do you want to drink?" I ask. My tongue trips a little over calling the two syllables and the fact that I'm referring to someone other than my mother as *Mama.*

"Water, please," she says. She's being awfully short with me. Did something happen?

I nod and glance around, looking for a place to get water. I catch sight of the sink—I've seen people drink from the sinks in movies. I go over to the sink, turning the handle to blue and flipping it up so that water begins to pour from the faucet. I fill up one glass, then the next, and the third. I take a hesitant sip from one of the glasses—it's not bad.

"What are you doing?" Aaron asks.

I freeze. "Getting a drink?"

"You got it from the faucet," he says.

"So?" I'm panicking. What is the big deal? Is the water in Vyctorya so bad that the people don't drink it? And if so, how did I not know that?

"You hate the water here," Melissa says, hands on her hips. "You make me buy water bottles every week at the grocery store."

"I, um—" What do I say? What do I say? "—thought I'd give it another try?"

Melissa huffs and shakes her head.

"Sorry?" I say, but Melissa doesn't say anything else. She picks up the pot of spaghetti and takes it over to the table. I take one of the other glasses and hand it over to Aaron, who still looks suspicious. Am I that bad of an actress? I pick up the other glasses and bring them to the table, setting them down at the place settings. I slide gratefully into my chair, hopeful that there won't be any more hard-hitting questions for the night.

My hope is quickly quashed.

"Why did you get out spoons?" Aaron asks.

"Because it's proper?" I try to keep the question out of my voice, but it doesn't work. I'm horribly confused. Do they not use spoons?

"Why would we need spoons for spaghetti?" Aaron doesn't let up.

"To gather the noodles." I grab a forkful of noodles and place them on a spoon, swirling them on it so that it's easier to eat. Aaron looks unimpressed.

"Since when do you eat like that?"

"Aaron, enough," Melissa says. I sigh in relief. She turns to me, suspicion on her face. "Are you feeling all right, Chava?"

"I'm fine," I say, voice a little high-pitched. "Why?"

"You just seem a little... off."

"Just... not feeling the best," I say. "But I'll get over it." I fight the urge to laugh, something I do when I'm nervous.

Melissa hums. "Take some medicine before you go to bed, then."

"I will," I lie, and breathe normally when everyone's attention leaves me and turns to the food. I've never been more grateful for spaghetti in my life.

I make it through the rest of dinner unscathed. Aaron rushes from the table as soon as we're done eating, and Melissa has a rule about cooking and cleaning that I get a little lost on. All I know is that I'm stuck doing dishes for the first time in my life.

"The dishwasher is dirty," Melissa says as she puts her plate in the sink.

I nod and look at the pile of dishes in the sink. Plates, forks, glasses, a pot. It's filled nearly to the brink, and I don't know how to clean any of it. Logically, I know that you use soap and warm water, but putting it into action—it seems like a herculean task.

Still, I have to do this. I roll up the sleeves of the denim jacket I have yet to take off and turn the tap to red before turning the water on. I watch for a moment as it fills up the tub and then begin my search for soap. I scour the counter for soap and see a plastic container full of some blue liquid. I pick that up and open the cap, squeezing experimentally. Bubbles pop out of the top.

"Huh," I say. I shrug and squeeze a line of the liquid into the sink. It immediately begins to foam up, a mountain of bubbles forming. My eyes widen, and I reach for the faucet, quickly turning the water off. Beside the faucet is a sponge, which I pick up. Bringing it to my nose, I sniff it and make a face. It smells old. Still, it's the only sponge I see, so I dip it into the water and pick up a plate, wiping off the sauce and other food debris stuck to it. I continue this process with the rest of the dishes, and when I'm done, I transfer them to the dishwasher.

Once the dishwasher is full, I stare at it for a minute, attempting to figure out how it works. I see the word "START" and press it, hoping for the best. Some lights flash green, and then rumbling emanates from the appliance. I sigh.

At least I can do one thing right.

A little before midnight, I get a phone call from an unknown caller.

"Hello?" I answer.

"Hey, it's me," Chava says.

I slump back in her bed, relieved. "Hi."

"So," Chava begins, dragging out the word. "We might have a slight problem."

"What's that?" I ask.

"Florence figured it out."

I sit back up. "What? How?"

"Something about a panic button?"

I reach for the button around my neck, my fingers stroking the smooth surface. It's disguised as a locket, but instead of pictures inside, there's a tracking chip. I'd never even thought about taking it off. That was my downfall.

Tears prick my eyes. "So, that's it then, huh? When is she coming to get me?"

"That's the thing…" Chava says. "She's not."

"Seriously?" I ask.

"Yeah, she said as long as you're safe and keep your panic button on you, then she won't interfere. She said that you needed this week."

"Yeah," I say softly. "I do."

"Why?" Chava asks. "I don't get why you're doing this. You're a princess—you have literally everything. Your bedroom is bigger than the apartment I grew up in."

I frown. "My life isn't just big bedrooms."

"Rooms, plural? You have more than one?"

"That's not what I meant." I sigh. "My life has been planned out since the day I was born. I just… I wanted some time to explore the world for myself."

"I call bullshit," Chava says.

My eyes widen. "Pardon?"

"You're risking everything for a few days to be 'normal?' No way. There's something you're not telling me."

I feel my face burn, even though Chava can't see me. "Well, what about you? You're the one who agreed to switch with me in the first place!"

Chava's silent on the phone for a minute. I've just started to worry that maybe she actually hung up on me when she speaks.

"You're not the only one who needed to get out of your life," she whispers.

"Is this about that fundraiser?"

Chava lets out a bitter chuckle. "Yeah, I probably should have mentioned that."

"What is it?"

"It's a fundraiser to earn money for brain cancer research. My mom organized it."

"But why?"

"Because… because my father had brain cancer. He was diagnosed when I was fifteen. He died last year." Chava's voice is thick.

"I—I'm so sorry," I say. "I had no idea."

"Yeah, well, now you do," Chava says. "So it's your turn. What are you getting out of this week?"

I fist my hand in the loose pajama shorts I'd put on. "It's… complicated."

"More complicated than my life? Did I mention I just broke up with my ex-girlfriend?"

I'm taken aback. "Are you… a lesbian?"

"Bisexual," Chava corrects. "Why does it matter?" She sounds defensive.

"It doesn't!" I hurry to assure her. "It's just—I *am* a lesbian."

"Oh," Chava says. "Then why are you marrying this duke guy?"

"Because no one knows," I tell her. "Well, no one but Florence."

"That makes sense," Chava says. "I wondered why she was so willing to go along with this."

"Yeah," I say. We sit in silence. I cross my legs and pick at a loose thread on Chava's blue comforter. After a moment, the phone buzzes in my ear. I look down to see a text message with a link to a dating website.

"What's this?" I ask, putting the phone on speaker.

I can practically hear Chava's smirk when she responds. "We're gonna get you a date."

# CHAPTER TEN
# CHAVA

I'M AWAKENED BY A PILLOW to the face. I shoot up in bed, convinced that I've been caught and am about to be thrown in the dungeon, only to find Florence standing at the end of the fourposter with her hands on her hips. I reach blindly for the phone on the nightstand and blink blearily at the time it shows.

"What are you doing?" I ask, a hint of a whine in my voice. "It's six-thirty."

"I know," Florence says. "I let you sleep in. Aisling's awake by six."

I flop back onto the mattress and groan. "Why the hell does she wake up at six in the morning?"

"She has yoga," Florence tells me.

I groan again. Of course, Aisling is one of those people. Why couldn't I have switched lives with someone who is as lazy as me?

"And? You want me to what?" I ask.

"Go to yoga," Florence says. "It's at seven, so you better get ready. I laid out the clothes for you in the closet. It's half an hour, then you'll need to come back here and change for breakfast. We're dining with the duke."

"This is hell," I mutter to the ceiling.

"Get dressed!" Florence calls over her shoulder. The door slams shut behind her. I sigh and get out of bed, walking over to the closet and putting on the clothes that have been picked out for me. I meet Florence outside, and she leads me to the palace gym—because of course the palace has a gym.

The next thirty minutes are a mixture of my worst high school gym memories and a brand new kind of torture that makes my thighs shake and my ankles burn. The trainer gives me a strange look and mutters something to Florence who shrugs and whispers something back.

Then, I'm being led back to Aisling's room, where yet another outfit has been laid out for me, this one a yellow sundress with a cream cardigan. I pull it on and slip on the heels. While I'm dressing, Florence speaks from the main room.

"I did some digging on you last night," she informs me. "Your mother is originally from Vyctorya. You have a younger brother. You attended a Jewish day school and received full marks until last year when your father died. Your mother moved you and your brother here, to Vyctorya, to move in with your maternal grandfather and enrolled you in the local international school. Unfortunately, your grades didn't match the standards you'd set back in America, and that affected your application to Purdue University, which rejected you. Did I get that right?"

I step out of the closet, rubbing my arm, feeling strangely bare. Florence raises an eyebrow.

"Yes," I say.

Florence nods. "You were a great student, Chava, and involved in a lot of extracurriculars. A shoo-in for Purdue University, really. But grief can really mess up a person's life."

I bite my lip hard enough to draw blood.

"I've called the Dean of the College of Engineering at Purdue. He's agreed to an interview with you on Wednesday afternoon," Florence says.

My mouth drops open, but before I can say anything, Florence grabs my arm and walks me down the halls to the dining room.

Florence glances at her watch as we approach a pair of large, wooden double doors. "Ugh, we're late." She steps forward and throws them open to reveal a long table made of some sort of dark wood. There are probably fifty chairs around the whole thing, but only three places are set at the end closest to the large windows that look out at the palace gardens. The table is empty.

My head is still reeling with the news about Purdue, but I have the strength of mind to remember where I'm at and what I'm supposed to be doing—and who I'm supposed to be fooling. "What about the king and queen?" I ask. Florence gives me a glare and ushers me to the seat at the head of the table.

"They have an early meeting today. I'll go let the chef know we're here." Florence turns and leaves without another word. I sigh and place my chin in my hands, my elbows on the table. It's horrible manners, but there is no one around to see. I look around the room—up at the crystal chandelier, at the floral arrangements spaced around the room, at the duke standing in the doorway. Oh, shit.

"I'm sorry I'm late," the duke says, hurrying toward the table. He easily slides into the seat to my right and runs a hand through his dark hair. "I went for a run and lost track of time."

"Ew." The word is out of my mouth before I can stop it. I've always hated running—the mile was my nemesis in high school—and the thought that anyone does it for fun astounds me. Still, Aisling might be one of those people, seeing as she wakes up at six in the morning to exercise. People like that are capable of anything.

Still, the duke doesn't seem offended. He throws his head back and laughs, exposing the length of his throat. His hair is loose today, falling in waves around his face. It's longer than I originally thought, long enough that he could put it up in a bun or a ponytail if he wanted.

"Not a runner?" the duke asks, his laughter subsiding.

"It depends on the day," I say diplomatically. Does Aisling run? Is that something I should have known?

"Well, maybe we can go for a run together, on the right day," the duke says.

I smile tightly. "Maybe."

The side door opens, and a kitchen server wheels a cart filled with breakfast food into the room. Florence follows shortly behind.

"I wasn't sure what you ate, so the chef made a little of everything," Florence says. She only trips a little when she sees that the duke is in the room, and she quickly recovers. "Good morning, Your Grace."

"Good morning," the duke returns. "I appreciate your care for my diet, but I'll eat whatever you put in front of me."

Florence laughs lightly, completely playing off the fact that she was talking to me. "Wonderful. I should introduce myself. I am Lady Florence Ahuja, Aisling's lady-in-waiting. You'll be seeing a lot of me."

"It's nice to meet you," the duke says. He stands up from his chair and reaches across the table to shake Florence's hand, who looks surprised at the treatment. "I'm Brennan, but I'm sure you knew that."

Florence smiles. "I did, Your Grace."

"Oh, you don't have to call me that. Call me Brennan."

"Maybe."

The kitchen server begins setting the plates from the cart onto the table: tarts and danishes, strawberries and orange slices, sausages, eggs, toast. It's like our own hotel buffet, and there's nearly as much food. Florence sits down once it's all laid out and quietly thanks the woman, who nods and takes the cart back through the side door. We sit for a moment; I stare at the food.

"Shall we?" Florence says, motioning toward the food. I grab a strawberry tart and some orange slices. I bite into an orange, trying my best to not let the juice drip down my chin. I imagine that Florence would have my head for that.

We eat quietly. I put some eggs on my plate and scoop some onto my fork. I don't look at Florence or the duke as I chew and hope they don't look at me, either. I eat quickly but as lady-like as I possibly can. I want this meal to be over with, so I can go hide back in Aisling's room once more. The longer I'm around the duke, the more likely I am to mess up and ruin Aisling's future.

Finally, Florence finishes and looks up to catch my eye. She notices my empty plate and nods.

"Well, Your Grace, I apologize for leaving you to dine alone, but Her Highness has many engagements for today in order to prepare for the wedding," Florence says, standing up.

I stand up, push my chair in, and make to leave.

"Have a good day," the duke says.

I pause and turn back. "You too." He smiles at me, and my stomach flips. Florence comes up beside me and grabs my arm, leading me out of the room.

"Thank God that's over with," I mutter.

Florence laughs. "Yes, now we just have several appointments to attend."

"Wait, what?" I stop. She turns to face me.

"There are things that need to get done before the wedding. You'll be attending to them. I just said that."

"I thought that was just an excuse to get out of there!"

"Sadly, no. First, we have to do a hair run—"

"A what?" What the hell is that?

Florence sighs. "The hair stylist is going to style your hair for the wedding, and we'll decide if it works or not."

"Why am I doing this?"

"Because," Florence hisses, stepping closer to me so she can be quiet, "it needs to be done, and Aisling isn't here to do it."

"All right, fine! Let's just get this over with."

Shortly after we arrive back in Aisling's room, a man breezes in, an arm sweeping ahead of him, as if clearing his path of all obstacles with his black, rhinestone-encrusted suitcase trailing behind him silently. The doors shut behind him as he comes to stand in the middle of the room, and his gray eyes twinkle as they look at me, sitting at the vanity. He smirks as he runs a hand through his black hair, styled in a pouf, that matches his all-black outfit, down to the polish on his nails, contrasting his pale, white skin.

"So," he says, rummaging through his bag and producing a comb, "*Your Highness*, what made you decide to chop off all your hair?"

"Luka." Florence's voice is a warning. He shrugs innocently and opens his suitcase, pulling out extensions the color of my hair.

"Do you… know something?" I ask nervously. How could he possibly know? I look at Florence, whose lips are pressed in a thin line. She nods once, as if saying that, *yes*, he does know. Did she tell him?

Luka winks at me, his gray eyes twinkling. "Don't worry, Your Highness. I know what secrets to keep, and you've already entrusted me with this one."

"Your job is to style hair and be quiet," Florence says.

Luka pouts. "Don't be like that, Flo."

"You're a flirt and a gossip," she snaps.

Luka catches my eye in the mirror and makes an exaggerated face. I can't help but crack a smile. Well, then, if there are no secrets in the room, I have a few questions of my own to ask.

"Why does Aisling have to get married anyway? Isn't she a little young?" I ask.

"It's a tradition for Vyctoryan royalty to be married by age eighteen," Florence says.

My eyebrows raise. "It sounds like an outdated tradition. Who gets married at eighteen?"

"I did," Florence says. I choke on air.

"You're married?" I splutter.

"I *was* married," Florence corrects. "Not anymore. I don't like to talk about it."

My mind spins with this new information: Who was she married to? What happened? Did her partner die, or did they leave?

A particularly hard yank in my hair brings me back to earth.

"Ouch, watch it," I tell Luka. He simply rolls his eyes and begins adding the extensions. I catch Florence's eye in the mirror.

"I still don't get this 'tradition,'" I say.

"I don't make the rules," she says. "I'm just here to help you follow them."

"Why the duke?" I ask, coughing slightly.

"Brennan Lewis took over the title of duke earlier this year," Florence says. "His father died back in January. The Duke of Belare has always had close ties to the royal family. The third son of Aisling's great-great-grandfather was gifted the land."

I wrinkle my nose. "So, they're like… related? Gross."

"She and Brennan are very distantly related," Florence agrees.

"Still. Gross."

"I didn't set up the match," Florence says. "The king and queen did."

I sit for a minute as Luka begins to style my hair, pulling out a curling iron and getting fearfully close to my face.

"What did you say happened to the duke's father?" I ask.

"I didn't." Florence taps at something on her phone, head tilted down.

"I didn't see anything about a duke dying on the news," I say. "It seems like that would be a big deal." If it was in January, we would have been here in Vyctorya. Granted, I didn't pay much attention to the news, but my government class had weekly current event quizzes. It seemed like the kind of question that would pop up.

"The media has an agreement with the Royal Family." Florence doesn't elaborate.

"But the duke isn't part of the Royal Family." I feel like an idiot, stating the obvious. The look that Florence gives me doesn't make me feel much more intelligent.

"This marriage has been in the works for a couple of years," she says. "The duke and his family have been under the same media gag order for just as long. Usually, there would be some sort of national service, but his death was…. It wasn't something we wanted to get out."

Luka whips me around to the mirror before I can say anything else. With a final flourish of hairspray, he gestures to my hair. It's piled on top of my head in a bun with tiny braids leading into it in strategic places. Certain pieces have been left to curl around my temples and cheeks.

Luka presses his cheek to mine, staring at me through the mirror.

"What do you think?" he asks.

"I'm not the one in charge," I say.

He huffs and turns to Florence. "Flo?"

Florence gets up from her seat and walks over to inspect my hair. She's silent as she scrutinizes Luka's work. Finally, she nods.

"Beautiful work, Luka, as usual," she tells him. Luka just smiles and gives me another wink before taking a few pictures and then starting to pack up his supplies. Florence turns my chair around and motions for me to stand up, which I do.

I sigh and scratch my head, which is beginning to itch. "But if the duke and Aisling have been engaged for a few years, how have they never met before?"

"She's been kept inside of the palace and out of the public eye since she was young," Florence says. She shrugs. "The king and queen never wanted to change that, even for a future husband."

I bite my lip, curiosity practically pouring from me. I'd never expected the palace to be so filled with secrets. Suddenly, I find myself filled with interest in Florence's past life and the duke's history.

I'd always been a sucker for mysteries.

# CHAPTER ELEVEN
# AISLING

I WAKE UP WHILE IT'S STILL dark out. I roll over and check Chava's phone—6:17 am. I've slept in. I sit up in bed, the comforter bunching around my waist, and stretch up, feeling my spine pop as it lengthens. I swing my feet out of bed and go over to Chava's closet in search of some active clothes. I grab a plain red t-shirt and a pair of shorts and pull those on, then the socks and tennis shoes. I'm not sure any of these necessarily qualify as "work-out clothes," but they're the closest I can find. I stick Chava's phone in the pocket of the shorts and make my way quietly downstairs and out the front door.

I set out on a light jog around the neighborhood, a slight thrill zinging through me as I realize I'm out in the open by myself for the first time in a long time—maybe forever. The streetlights blink on as I pass underneath them, lighting up the sidewalk. I have no music to listen to, and I have no one to talk to, so instead, I think about my plans for the week, which are admittedly abysmal. I have no idea what a "normal" life looks like, let alone how to go about one.

I make another couple of laps around the neighborhood before slowing to a stop in front of Chava's house. The sky is lightening now, and I check the phone to see that it's nearly seven o'clock. I take a deep breath and stretch my legs, letting my breathing even out as my heart rate slows back to normal. I head back inside, going straight to the kitchen for a glass of water. I grab a glass and fill it to the brim, downing it in a few gulps. I place the empty glass in the sink and turn so that my back rests against the counter.

Aaron stands in the doorway.

I jump. "Jesus Christ!"

Aaron cocks his head. "What are you doing?"

"What are you doing?" I can't get into a back-and-forth with this kid right now. My brain isn't in it.

"I asked you first," Aaron says. He squints his eyes at me. "Did you go for a run? You hate running."

"I'm trying new things," I say defensively. Apparently, I should've checked with Chava about what her hobbies were.

"You're acting weird."

"Yeah? Well, so are you."

*Great come back, Aisling.*

Aaron huffs and turns to leave. I feel a twinge of guilt.

"Wait!" I call out. Aaron turns back, his arms crossed over his chest. I realize how little he is, only coming up to my shoulder. "I'm sorry, Aaron. You're right, I have been acting weird. It's just… a weird week."

"Because of Papa?" Aaron asks. I latch onto this excuse.

"Yeah, because of Papa," I agree.

Aaron nods sadly. "I can't believe it's been a year."

"Yeah," I say softly, my heart hurting for this boy who lost his father too soon. Hesitantly, I add, "But we still have each other." Aaron stares at me for a minute strangely then turns to leave. I sigh, leaning my forehead against the doorway. How many more ways can I screw this up?

After deciding that I need to get out of Chava's house, I look up coffee shops near me. On all of the television shows, the character hangs out in coffee shops; maybe I'll find my first kiss there. I manage to find my way to *Espresso Yourself* from Chava's house. I walk through the front door, the bell overhead signaling my entrance. At the counter, the girl from yesterday, Emilia—Chava's ex-girlfriend—looks up and smiles when she sees me.

"Hey! What are you doing here?" she asks.

"Uh," I stumble for an excuse, and I notice her face fall. Is she going to yell at me like she did yesterday? "I wanted to talk to you."

Emilia brightens a little at this, though her expression is still guarded. "Oh, okay. Well, I'm done in ten, so go ahead and sit down, and I'll be out shortly."

For a second, I freeze, faced with all the possible tables. I force myself to relax and choose a table in the corner. While I wait for Emilia to get done with her shift, I study her under the terrible lighting in the cafe.

Emilia moves behind the counter with the grace of a dancer. I watch as she smiles at the customers who come up to her and handles their drinks with ease, calling out their names cheerfully. She glances over at me every once in a while. When she catches my eye, I blush and look down at the table.

A little panicked, I scan through Chava's phone for clues about Emilia. I'd asked about her while Chava was helping me set up the dating app, but all she'd told me was that they'd recently broken up and that Emilia was her best friend. It seemed complicated to me, but I wasn't going to say that.

I click on Chava's Instagram and go to her profile, scrolling through the pictures. There aren't many. The most recent one is of Chava and Emilia in prom dresses, arms around each other, radiating happiness. My throat tightens at the ease on their faces, the way they hold each other close. I look for another picture.

The next one is a happy birthday message to Aaron, featuring a picture of the boy himself glaring at the camera. The third one is a grainy picture of a man holding a toddler. I open up the post and read the caption: *I'll love you always, Papa.* There are several other pictures, showcasing Chava as she grew older with the man, her father. The last picture is one of Chava sitting next to her dad in a hospital bed, holding up peace signs, her screensaver. The date is from almost exactly a year ago, which holds up. Chava said the fundraiser on Wednesday was the one-year anniversary of her father's death. The post has 512 likes and 73 comments. Out of curiosity, I click into the comments.

*Brain cancer sucks*, writes one person.

*Tell your mom to let me know if she needs anything*, says another.

*Your papa was a great man. He will be greatly missed :'(*

"Hey!" Emilia says, sliding into the seat next to me. Hurriedly, I shut the phone off and place it face down on the table. She hands me a paper cup and takes a sip of her own. I let out a quick sigh of relief and take a drink. Bitterness floods my tongue, and I fight the urge to make a face. Apparently, Chava takes her coffee black.

I lick my lips and place the coffee down on the table, wondering if I can get away with not finishing it—or taking another drink at all.

"I'm really glad you came," Emilia says. I nod and debate picking the coffee back up just so I don't have to come up with an answer to that question. "I know yesterday was a little… weird." She pauses, as if to give me time to respond. I remember, suddenly, that I'd come into the coffee shop yesterday, and she'd thought I was Chava.

"Oh! Right!" I grab my drink and take a long pull, wincing at the taste. When I put it back down on the table, Emilia stares at me strangely. "I, uh, had a… um…"

Emilia says nothing. She clearly isn't going to let me out of this.

"I was just a little… stressed… about the… fundraiser," I say finally.

Emilia's shoulders slump, and she leans her head back. "I wondered."

"Mmhmm." What else am I supposed to say?

"You know I'm here for you." She looks at me, but I look at her hands, holding her coffee cup. One finger traces the rim of it. Her nails are long, perfect ovals painted an electric blue.

I sit in silence and try not to stare at her. She's painfully beautiful—her full mouth, her brown eyes, her pink hair. It's pulled back again, but there are two strands framing her face like a picture. My heart beats unbearably loud, and I pray that she can't hear it.

"I know this fundraiser isn't what you wanted," Emilia says, "but I'll be with you every step of the way. Things don't have to be weird just because we broke up."

It seems strange. In every movie or television show I've watched, when two people break up, they never want to see each other again. But when Chava first mentioned Emilia, there wasn't heartbreak in her voice; instead there was something closer to melancholy. And here is Emilia, urging me—Chava, I suppose—to lean on her.

"I guess I just… don't know what to expect," I say. It's the truth. This fundraiser—I have no idea who will be there or what kind of event it is. Anyone I can have in my corner, I'll take, and something tells me that Emilia is someone you want fighting for you.

Emilia smiles reassuringly, eyes crinkling. "It'll all work out, Chava. I know it will." I'm mesmerized, pinned down by her gaze. I've never been one to feel like I'm floating, but locking eyes with Emilia, I know that I'd never have to worry about that. She'd keep her hand in mine, and my feet would stay firmly on the ground.

Emilia coughs a little and looks back down at her cup. "Got any plans for the day?"

"Not really," I say.

"Well, since I'm going with you to the fundraiser, I suppose I need an outfit," Emilia says.

"Oh." My brow furrows. "Where do you want to go?"

"Well, Gracelynn's is the place to go for a dress," Emilia begins. My heart stops at the name—Gracelynn's? as in, the Gracelynn who designed and made my wedding dress?—but Emilia continues before I can spiral. "But I had something different in mind."

I sit in a wooden chair, one of many lined up against the wall. On the opposite wall are three dressing rooms. I watch the second door as clothing items drop to the floor around Emilia's feet. She pulls a pair of pants up her legs and then opens the door. She steps out, hand still on the doorknob, and strikes a pose.

"What do you think?" she asks. The suit is charcoal gray. The fabric of the pants hug her legs while the matching coat is a little baggy. She only wears a black tank top under the jacket, exposing the swell of her breasts.

"It's nice," I say, my cheeks warming.

She frowns. "You said that about the last two suits. Is it nicer than those ones?"

The previous two consisted of a bright blue suit that reminded me of something Florence would wear and a black suit with wide pant legs. All of them looked nice on her—too nice. I was surprised I hadn't exploded into a ball of flames yet.

"Obviously, I won't wear this tank top," Emilia says, holding the jacket away from her so that I can see the curve of her waist. "I've got a nice silvery, silk blouse that I thought I'd wear. Damn, we should have stopped by my house, so I could grab it."

"Will the silver go with the gray?" I ask.

Emilia pauses her rambling. "Good point." She shucks off the jacket and reaches for the button on her pants as if to undo them out here.

"Shouldn't you change in the dressing room?" I ask. I hate that my voice squeaks. "You're in the middle of a store."

"There's no one else here," Emilia complains, but the sales associate who'd greeted us when we first walked in steps into the hallway and she retreats back into the stall. The man has his nose upturned, and his face bears the expression of having smelled something distasteful. He glances at me, eyes lingering on my face, before turning and heading back into the store proper. I let out a sigh of relief.

When we'd first walked in half an hour ago, he'd looked me up and down and said, "You look like the princess."

I'd frozen, but Emilia had laughed and nudged me with her shoulder.

"She gets that a lot," she'd said, "but Chava was born and raised in the USA. Hey, isn't there a song that says that?"

"Uh, yeah." I had no idea if there was a song that sang that.

The man furrowed his brow but continued with his introduction of Renaldo's Atelier for Men. He'd been less than pleased when he learned that we were there for Emilia, but he'd shut his mouth and let us search.

"Ugh," Emilia groans in the dressing room. "There's nothing fun here. Everything is so boring!"

"We can go somewhere else," I offer.

"No, this is the only place fancy enough. I can find something, I know it. And besides, it's a memorial, not a fashion show. I don't need to stand out," she says.

"Do they not have a place for women's suits? Maybe that would make it easier to find something?"

"No. Don't you remember? We couldn't find suits anywhere for Final Formal."

I wrinkle my nose. Is Final Formal supposed to be like Prom? Could they really just not call it Prom?

"I know, I know," Emilia sighs. "Final Formal is still a dumb name for Prom, but I'm not the one who came up with it!" There's shuffling from behind the door, probably her rifling through the ten or so options she'd taken into the room with her.

I wonder what *Final Formal* had been like for Emilia and Chava. I wonder what it had looked like and where it had been and what songs had been played. Had they held hands as they walked into the room? Had they danced together under the lights? Had it been a good night, one worth remembering, or had it ended in disaster like it had in so many American TV shows I'd seen?

"Ooh! This is it!" *Bang!* "I'm fine!"

"What happened?" I ask. Under the door, Emilia dances from foot to foot, her striped socks slipping around.

"Just hit the door," Emilia tells me. "I'm good." The door swings open, and Emilia follows it, leaning her back against the wood. "How do I look?"

This suit is cut the same way as the gray one, but it's stark black. I wonder what makes this one stand out against all the other options, but she does look pretty in it.

"Great!" I say. "It'll look good with your top."

"Definitely," Emilia agrees. She pulls at a little white tag that's hanging from her armpit and grimaces.

"What?" I ask.

"The price," she says. "My mum would kill me if she knew I was spending this much."

I frown. "Is it a lot?"

"Yeah, but it's fine." Emilia glances down the hallway and takes a step closer so that she can lean down to whisper in my ear. "I'll just keep the price tags on and return it after the fundraiser."

Emilia heads back into the dressing room before I can say anything else. I wonder how much the suit costs. I wonder how much Emilia considers *expensive*. I wonder how much *I* would consider expensive.

# CHAPTER TWELVE
# CHAVA

After lunch, we meet in the formal dining room, where plates of cake are already placed on the table. A man stands at the head of the table, talking to the duke, though he looks to the door when Florence and I walk in.

"Your Highness!" the man smiles as I make my way toward the two of them. "I was just talking to His Grace about the cakes we have for you to taste. He knows his stuff."

I look over to the duke. His hair is a little damp, curling over his temples, and he wears a white button-up with black slacks. His hands are shoved into his pockets.

"That's, er, wonderful," I say. "You'll have to show him around the kitchen."

"You're welcome any time, Your Grace," he says to the duke.

The duke smiles. "Thank you, I appreciate that."

"Her Highness comes into the kitchens all of the time, mostly to sneak cookies," the man says. He looks to me with a secret smile, one that speaks of endearment.

"Okay, Leo, why don't we get started with the tasting?" Florence cuts in.

The man, Leo, laughs. "Of course, of course. First up, we have chocolate raspberry." He gestures to the plate closest to him. I let my eyes scan the table and count nearly twenty plates with two thin slices of cake on each. Florence steers me over by the duke, and Leo hands us both forks.

"Please, try some," the chef says. He motions for us to sit down, pulling out my chair. I slide into it with a quiet *thank you*. I chance a glance at the duke, and he's staring right back at me. I will my cheeks to stay a normal color and reach forward to cut off a piece of the cake before bringing it to my mouth. I chew slowly, doing my best to keep my face neutral. The chocolate is good, and the cake itself is moist, but I hate raspberry.

"Thoughts?" Leo asks.

"Um…" Does the princess like chocolate raspberry? Would she want her wedding cake to be this flavor? Why hadn't they already picked out the flavor of the stupid wedding cake by now?

"It's good," the duke says, "but I've never been a huge fan of raspberries."

Leo waves a hand. "Of course. Well, the next one is rather plain, just a white cake with buttercream frosting. I almost didn't make it an option, but it is a classic."

Leo and the duke continue to debate the cakes as the afternoon rolls along. I dutifully slice off chunks of cake and stuff them in my mouth. Some are delicious; others make me wince. I do my best to hide my every reaction because I don't know the princess's tastes, and I don't want to tip off the chef or mislead the duke.

This *pretending to be a princess* thing is more difficult than I'd originally thought.

"The last one," Leo says, "is a devil's food cake. I had to sneak it in there for you, Your Highness."

I perk up. Finally, an idea of what the princess likes.

"Oh, uh, thank you, Leo," I say. I scoop up some cake, eager for this afternoon to be over. The cake is rich and creamy. Out of all the elaborate flavors I've had the past couple of hours, this one tastes the best.

"So, is this the one?" the duke asks while I'm still chewing. I cover my mouth with my hand and look at Florence. She nods minutely.

"Do you like it?" I ask once I've swallowed, letting my hand fall to my lap.

He gives me a smile that turns into a laugh. My stomach flips at the sound.

"You've, uh, got some…" The duke wipes at the corner of his lip. My hand covers my mouth so quickly that I slap myself in the face. I face the table, wanting nothing more than to hide my head in the cloth, as I wipe at my mouth.

"Devil's food it is!" Leo declares.

Florence descends on me before I can say anything else.

"Thank you so much for your time, gentlemen," Florence says, grabbing my arm and practically lifting me out of the chair. "Her Highness has something to attend to before dinner."

"Wait, please," the duke says, standing up. He looks at me. Is it my imagination, or are his cheeks a little red? "I was wondering if you'd like to do something with me tonight?"

"Tonight?" I ask. I look over at Florence, who nods. I turn back to him. "Like… what?"

"I saw the wickets for croquet while I was running this morning," he says. "Do you play?"

"Uh, yes?" *No!*

The duke smiles. "Great. Then, croquet?"

"Croquet," I agree.

"Why did I agree to croquet?" I complain to Florence as she leads me to the back of the palace. Throughout dinner, I'd tried to look up the rules on Aisling's phone under the table, but nothing had stuck. I just have to hope Aisling is horrible at the game.

The duke is already at the lawn by the time Florence and I arrive. He gives me a small smile.

"Good evening, Your Highness," the duke says, bowing.

"Good evening," I reply. I don't add his title because I don't know it. The closest I can think of is *your dukeness*, and I know that's not right.

"Thank you for coming," he says after a moment of awkward silence.

"Of course," I say after Florence shoots me a look. "I'd like to get to know you."

Something flashes across his face, but it's gone before I can make it out. He gives me a polite smile instead and waves a hand at the lawn.

"Shall we, then?" he asks. I glance at Florence, but she's no longer beside me.

"Florence?" I ask, a hint of panic in my tone. I spin around, searching for her, but she's only a few feet away, talking on her phone. "Where are you going?"

"I'm afraid there's some business with the wedding I need to attend to," Florence says, giving me a warning look.

"You're leaving us alone?" My voice goes up a pitch, and I work to bring it down. "That's allowed?" I figured the crown princess would need a chaperone, like in the movies.

"You're on the palace grounds, Your Highness," Florence says. There's a warning in her voice now, too. Still, she doesn't seem pleased to be leaving me alone with the duke.

"Right, right," I say, glancing at the man in question.

"Good luck," Florence says before taking her leave. I don't know if she means for the game or for me in general. Either way, I know I'll need it. Nevertheless, I take a breath and ready myself. I have a croquet game to play and a duke to impress.

I turn to him, pasting a big smile on my face. "Let's play."

I go to the rack and grab the first mallet I see. It takes me a minute to pull the stupid thing from the rack; I somehow nearly fall over in the process. He's too polite to laugh. Once we have our mallets and balls set in place, the duke gestures for me to go first. I step forward and hit my ball with the mallet. There's a loud *crack!* when the two items connect, and the ball shoots across the lawn.

The duke steps forward and hits his own ball. We do this a few times, unbearably silent. Neither of us tells the other "good shot" or any other words of encouragement. Hell, I'd settle for him teasing me for being terrible, which I must be if he can't cobble together an affirmative phrase.

When it's my turn next, I line up my shot and swing— perhaps a little too hard. The ball goes flying and ricochets off a nearby tree. I drop to the ground as it shoots back at me and rest my forehead on the grass for a moment, two, wishing I could just sink into the dirt and become a worm. It wouldn't matter if I got into Purdue if I was a worm.

Above me, there's a strangled sort of sound. I look up to see the duke has dropped his mallet, one hand covering his mouth while his other arm is wrapped around his middle. As my gaze meets his, he seems to lose whatever battle he was fighting. He leans over completely, laughter spilling up and out. I grin wryly and get to my feet.

"Bad day, I guess," I say as his laughter subsides.

"You're worse than my sister, and she trips over her ball at least once a game," he says, still chuckling. "No offense, Your Highness."

I'm too relieved to feel offended. Laughter, I can work with.

"How old is your sister?" I ask.

"Twelve," he tells me.

"Well, then, I can't be too embarrassed," I say. "Twelve is a very wise age. My brother—" I cut myself off. "I'm sorry—my *friend's* brother is thirteen. He's very smart." *When he's not being the most annoying person on the planet,* I add silently.

"I bet your friend would say otherwise," the duke says. "Little siblings can be the worst. The best, but also the worst."

"Do you just have the one sister?"

"No, I have another," he says. "She's eight."

"Surrounded by girls, huh?"

"I suppose, but it's never been a bother. I mean, I was nearly halfway through my childhood by the time Cece was born."

"Do they gang up on you now?" I ask. Keeping the conversation on him means less of a chance for me to screw up.

"No, they use me to gang up on each other. Lots of games of 'War,'" he says, a fond smile gracing his lips. He has a nice smile.

"The card game?" I ask, banishing the thought from my mind.

"No, we put on makeshift armor and chase each other around the house," he clarifies. I let out a snort at the mental image. He regales me with tales of War as we finish our game. I assume he wins, but I can't tell. But by the time he goes to shake my hand, Florence has reappeared.

"Good game…" I hesitate again, unable to remember his title once more.

"You can call me Brennan," he says quickly. "We will be married in a few days, after all."

That's a smack to the face, as silly as it is. For a moment, I'd forgotten I was pretending. So I tell him, "Then, you should call me Aisling."

"It was a pleasure talking with you, Aisling," Brennan says, pausing at the princess's name. Is it my imagination, or does he take his time with the syllables?

"I had a wonderful time, Brennan," I reply. He smiles when I say his name—bright, brilliant, beautiful. I can't help but smile back.

# CHAPTER THIRTEEN
# AISLING

The next morning is a flurry of activity. Melissa and Gian leave early in the morning to go to the venue of the fundraiser, leaving me alone with Aaron. I go downstairs to the kitchen for breakfast and find Chava's brother sitting at the table, a bowl in front of him.

"Good morning," I say cheerfully. Aaron's been giving me weird looks constantly, so I figure there's not much more I can do to mess anything up. I might as well go all in. "What are you having?"

There's the strange look again. "Cereal." The *duh* in his voice is palpable.

Cereal. I've never had it before—the palace chef has always made my meals from scratch. "I know that. I meant what kind of cereal?"

Aaron ignores me and takes another bite from his spoon. I blow out a breath and turn to the cabinets.

Yesterday, after I'd gotten back from the cafe with Emilia, I'd done some snooping around the kitchen to acquaint myself. I head for the pantry, a plain wooden door that I hadn't paid any attention to at first glance. Now, I knew that it housed food.

I step inside the pantry and look around for something to eat. There's a loaf of bread, but I don't trust myself to try and work the toaster. A yellow box catches my eye— Cheerios. *Made with 100% whole grain oats.* I pick it up for a closer look. The little round pieces are in what looks to be a bowl, a bit of milk splashing out of the side. This must be the cereal that Aaron's eating.

I take the box out into the kitchen with me and pick out a bowl before opening the fridge to grab the milk. I set it all on the counter, pouring first the cereal and then the milk. I put the milk back in the fridge and grab a spoon before heading over to the table.

I sit down beside Aaron and scoop up some Cheerios. They wobble in a big pile in the dip of my spoon. I carefully place them in my mouth and chew slowly.

"You're not Chava," Aaron says.

I choke on the Cheerios.

"W-what?" I cough out. I can't stop coughing. Aaron stands up and hits me in between my shoulder blades a couple of times. I clutch at my chest, gasping in breath. Finally, once my windpipe is clear, I turn to gape at Aaron, tears in the corners of my eyes from my near-death experience.

"What did you say?" I demand again. Aaron eyes me calmly.

"You're not Chava," he repeats.

I take a deep breath. I can play this off. "And what makes you think that?"

"Chava is lactose-intolerant."

Shit. The memory hits me like a truck: *"I can't drink milk," Chava says. "I don't eat cheese either, but sometimes I'll eat ice cream. It usually makes my stomach hurt, though, which my mom knows, so make sure you escape to my room if you eat it." I type the information into the Notes app, but I'm not concerned. Ice cream isn't my favorite thing in the world. It shouldn't be a problem.*

It's a problem.

I stare up at Aaron in horror. He seems to loom over me in my seat, arms crossed across his chest and a knowing little smirk pulling at the corners of his mouth. Soon, though, the smugness drops and is replaced with something else.

"Where's my sister?" he asks. For the first time since I've known him, Aaron seems unsure. Uncertain. And maybe a little scared.

"She's safe," I tell him. "Nothing's wrong." I don't know how much I should be sharing with this thirteen-year-old. How much can I give without being found out completely? A new thought strikes me: is he going to tell his mother?

"Who are you?" Aaron demands.

"My name is Aisling," I say. That's innocent enough. Lots of people are probably named Aisling. Isn't it a trend to name your baby after royals? I think I read that in an article that always circulates when it's nearing my birthday.

"Who are you?" he repeats. I look at him in confusion. He sighs, exasperated. I can see why Chava needed a break.

"I'm a friend of your sister's," I tell him. "A new friend. We just met, actually."

"How do you look so much like her?" Aaron asks. He moves back to his seat but continues to eye me as if he doesn't trust me.

I shrug. "I don't know. It's new to me, too."

"But why are you here?"

This kid won't let up.

"A secret mission," I say quietly, acting like it's something special.

The glare he levels me with is unimpressed. "I'm thirteen, not three."

"Fair enough. I'm here because I—" I choke. Why could I share my secret so easily with Chava, but I can't force the words out now? But, I suppose, it's a secret because I don't go around sharing it. It's personal and private and terrifying. There's still the possibility that Aaron will send this all crumbling around my head. I need a different approach.

"Because Chava wanted… space," I say instead. I wince a little at the fact that I'm airing out Chava's inner feelings, but if anyone could understand her grief, wouldn't it be her little brother?

Aaron cocks his head quizzically. "Space?"

"She needed room to breathe and… grieve," I finish softly.

"She needed to grieve without us?" Aaron sounds hurt. I quickly backtrack.

"That's not it, no," I say, though I guess it kind of is. "She just doesn't really agree with the fundraiser that your mom is holding, and she wanted to get away from it all. You know, grief hits us all in different ways. I think the way your mom is handling it is stressful to Chava, and she wanted space to handle it her way."

"But what about my way?" Aaron demands. I'm horrified to see there are tears in his brown eyes.

"What do you mean?" I ask.

"What if my way to grieve is with my family? What if I need her?"

I blink, shocked. "I don't think she realized. I don't think Chava would have done this if she'd known that."

Aaron scrubs angrily at his eyes. "Well, I do. I want her back. Bring her back."

My throat closes up. This can't be happening. I can't be stuck between these two choices, a few days of freedom and a grieving boy who wants his sister.

"Aaron—"

"What's in it for you, anyway?" he demands. "What are you getting out of this?"

"A chance to be myself," I say quietly. Aaron sniffles once, but his face is cooling from red back to his natural coloring.

"What does that mean? You're the princess. Can't you do anything you want?"

"How did you know I'm the princess?"

"You have the same name as the princess. I'm thirteen, not three," he says again.

I suppose that that's fair. I sigh. "I may be the princess, but that doesn't mean I can do anything I want. Chava and I—we saw an opportunity, and we took it. If you really want, I'll call her right now, and we'll switch back. But I'm going to be honest with you. I need this week. I really, truly do. And Chava needs it, too."

Aaron stares at me, unblinking and unchanging. I shift uncomfortably in my seat. Finally, he nods.

"Fine," he says.

"Really?"

"Yeah. If this is what Chava wants, then I won't say anything. But she owes me big time. And so do you."

"You have a favor of the Crown Princess of Vyctorya," I tell him.

He makes a face. "That's weird to hear coming out of my sister's mouth."

"Can you tell a difference between us at all? Other than the mannerisms, I suppose." I'm curious. He's one of the closest people to Chava; if he can't see a difference, then who could?

Aaron squints heavily at my face. "You have a zit on your chin."

The gray dress fits wonderfully, as I knew it would. Gracelynn is the best seamstress in the city—perhaps in all of Vyctorya.

The bodice hugs my chest well, held up with spaghetti straps, and the rest of the material flows out into a cloudy skirt. I twirl around in the mirror, loving the way the fabric swirls around my knees.

"Chava wouldn't do that." Aaron is in the doorway. I let out a little shriek, caught off guard. I put a hand to my chest and glare at him.

"What do you mean?" I ask.

"You're acting like a princess," he tells me. "Chava doesn't act like a princess."

My cheeks burn a little. "Well, I was just looking at the dress."

"Chava doesn't like wearing fancy dresses."

"Okay?"

"So don't act happy about wearing the dress."

I wish that Aaron hadn't figured me out, mostly because he's very judgmental of my ability to portray his sister. I cross my arms over my chest.

"I won't," I say. Aaron gives me an unimpressed look but leaves. I walk over and shut the door behind him, then turn back to the mirror.

Chava doesn't have much in the way of makeup— some concealer and a tube of cheap mascara that I can tell will smudge if I so much as sweat—but Melissa had dropped off a bag of makeup before I'd put on the dress with an order to put on some lipstick and eyeshadow.

I dump the bag out on Chava's dresser and begin to sift through the makeup. There's a small palette of warm brown tones that I pick out and a bright red lipstick that will really pop against the gray of the dress. I carefully set about making up my face, holding the tiny sponge brush that comes with the eyeshadow and dabbing it on my eyelids.

Chava's phone dings as I'm putting the finishing touches on my lipstick. It's probably her, checking in to see how I'm doing. I walk over to the nightstand and grab it, turning it on.

It's Emilia.

My stomach does a somersault. I blink quickly and shake my head, willing myself to calm down. It's just a text, not a declaration of love. Not that I need a declaration of love from Emilia; I only just met the girl.

I resist the urge to smack myself. I'm being ridiculous. I type in Chava's passcode and open up the message.

**Em<3:** its still cool to meet u at the fundraiser right?

Another message comes in as I'm typing up a response.

**Em<3:** i don't need to stop u and ur mom from killing each other?

**Me:** No, we're fine. I'll see you at the event.

I pause before typing out another response, one that I'm sure Chava would send to Emilia if she were here.

**Me:** Thank you for doing this.

**Me:** You have no idea how much it means to me.

**Em<3:** of course :*

I sigh, trying to fight the smile that begs to overtake my face. I shouldn't be giggling like this over Emilia. In fact, I should check the dating app. That's why I downloaded it in the first place.

In the app, I find that several people have matched with me. My heart leaps, and I smile, a little giddy. All of these people like me, at least enough to swipe on me. I open the message that I'd gotten a notification for, from a girl named Hallie.

**Hallie:** Hey.

I pause and bite my lip, but eventually type, *Hey*, back. That's cool, right?

**Hallie:** Anyone ever tell you that you look like the princess?

I huff out a laugh. Apparently, that happened to Chava a lot.

**Me:** All the time.

**Hallie:** So, what do you do for fun?

**Me:** I like movies.

**Hallie:** Movies are nice.

Banging on Chava's door interrupts my conversation.

"Chava, we need to leave!" Melissa says.

"One second!" I call back. Quickly, I send a goodbye message to Hallie and slip the phone into my dress pocket. I hurry over the door and open it. Melissa still stands there, and her eyes widen when she sees me.

"Um, ready?" I say.

Melissa nods and turns to leave, but just as quickly, she turns back. "You look beautiful."

It's the softest she's sounded with me since I've taken over Chava's life.

"Oh, uh, so do you," I say, and smile. She leaves without smiling back.

# CHAPTER FOURTEEN
# CHAVA

**Chava:** We have a small problem.

It's weird to see my name attached to a message sent to me, but Aisling and I had both agreed to put each other's names in the case either of our phones were unlocked.

My breathing speeds up at her message. I'm already a mess of emotions today; how could it possibly get worse?

The phone begins to ring in my hand, and I answer it.

"What's the problem?" It's not the most polite way to answer a call, and I could probably be thrown into a dungeon for talking to a princess like that, but I'm too stressed to care.

"Aaron knows," Aisling says.

My eyes close. "Shit."

"But it's okay!" she insists.

"My little brother, one of only three, maybe four, people that you had to convince you were me, figured out you're actually not me. How is it okay?" I demand.

"He promised not to tell anyone," Aisling says. I sigh. It's painfully obvious she doesn't have siblings.

"What does he want?" I ask. With Aisling's resources, I can't imagine any of his demands would be out of reach, but they could be inconvenient.

"He just wants to talk to you," she says.

"What?"

"Here."

There's some shuffling and muttering on the other side of the phone before my brother's voice fills my ear. "Hey."

"Aaron, I know this all probably sounds crazy, but I'm begging you—"

"I'm not going to tell Mama," Aaron cuts me off. "Or anyone, for that matter."

I pause. "Why?"

"You haven't been the same since Papa died," he says. A pang jolts through me at his words. *One year today, he died one year ago today.* "I know it's hard. It's really hard. And it sucks that you're not here for it. But if this is what you need to do, then do it."

"This isn't just about me. I'm doing this for Aisling, too," I tell him.

"That's what she told me."

There's silence, as if he doesn't know what to say or maybe he's preparing to say something.

"You'll be back soon, right?" Aaron's voice is small, sounding like his age for the first time in a long time. He grew up fast after our father died.

"Yeah, on Friday," I say, nodding even though he can't see me.

"Okay." Uncertainty colors his tone, but I'm confident in our plan.

"Are you going to be okay today?" I ask. Aaron was never supposed to know we switched. It should've been like I was there with him the entire day. For a moment, I'm wracked with guilt. Maybe I should've sucked it up and been there with my family.

"Yeah," Aaron says. "Are you?"

I look down at the comforter I'm sitting on, picking at a loose thread in the fabric. I wonder if I should mention it to Florence, so it can be replaced. It doesn't bother me, but I can't imagine the princess sleeps on anything less than the best the country has to offer.

"I'll be fine," I say. "I have a meeting with the dean of engineering at Purdue. Aisling had it set up for me."

"Oh. Cool." Aaron pauses. "Can we do something together? When you get back?"

Tears sting my eyes. "Of course. I... I love you."

"I love you, too."

I can't remember the last time Aaron said those words to me. At least a year, maybe longer.

I hang the phone up. Tears drip down my cheeks and stain the white blanket below me. I take a deep breath, then push the heels of my hands into my eyes. My meeting is at three PM. I have to hold it together until then.

My meeting with the dean comes far too quickly, and yet, it seems like it takes a million years at the same time. I want to get it over with, but at the same time, I need it to last forever. I need to make an impression. This is my future.

I click on the Zoom link sent to my email and sit back on the princess' couch. Florence had brought me a laptop, and I'd set it up on the table, dressed in a black dress with a Peter Pan collar. For the first time since I started pretending to be the princess, I'm glad to raid her closet.

The Zoom meeting loads, sending me to a waiting room. I fight to control my breathing, my fingers tapping incessantly on my knee. I stare at my face on the screen, making sure there's no stray piece of food or makeup or hair. There's not; I look perfect, too perfect, maybe, but maybe it's perfect enough to get me into Purdue.

Finally, I'm let into a meeting, and then the dean of engineering at Purdue University stares at me through his computer screen, halfway across the world, behind his large mahogany desk. He smiles congenially, hands folding in front of him.

"Hello, I assume I'm speaking to Miss Chava Burke?" he says.

"Yes," I say, praying my voice isn't higher than normal. "I'm Chava Burke."

"It's wonderful to meet you, Ms. Burke," the dean says. "Lady Ahuja had many great things to say about you when she asked to set up this interview. I'll admit—I don't usually do this, but she'd insisted that we were missing out on you."

My heart sings. I could kiss her.

*Thank you, Florence.*

"Thank you, sir," I say. "I appreciate you giving me a chance."

"Of course. So, Ms. Burke, tell me about yourself."

I launch into the tirade I've practiced, mentioning how my father is an alumni and how it's always been my dream to go to Purdue for engineering. I tell him about the activities I did back in America—golf and piano and any Academic Bowl I could squeeze into. I talk about my AP classes and scores. I talk about what I want to do with my degree, the things I want to create and make better.

"That's all very nice, Ms. Burke," the dean says, "but I want to hear about you in particular. I read all these things in your admissions essay. But what do you do for fun, not for an essay?"

"Um." I rack my brain. I'd had a speech planned, and I'd given it, but now he wanted more. Hadn't I talked about myself enough? What more could he want? "I liked to build cars with my father."

"Liked? Not anymore?" the dean asks.

I let out a shaky breath. "He, um, he died. Last year. Brain cancer."

The dean's face turns sympathetic. "Oh, I'm sorry. I didn't realize."

"That's why I moved to Vyctorya," I tell him, even though he hadn't asked. "That's why my grades slipped. I was… I was in a bad place for a long time where nothing seemed to matter. I kind of gave up on my dream, I'll admit. But I wish I hadn't. It *is* what I want. Things *do* matter. My dad would want me to keep going, no matter what. I wish I hadn't forgotten that."

The dean is silent for a moment, staring at me. His phone rings, and he glances at it and frowns.

"If you can excuse me for a moment, Ms. Burke." He mutes the meeting and his camera. I watch the blank screen, willing him to come back, hoping he'll let me finish my interview. After what feels like centuries but is only a minute according to the clock, he's back.

"Ms. Burke, I am so sorry, but I'm afraid there's an emergency I must attend to," he says.

"Oh, of course." My heart deflates. "Did you want to reschedule or—"

"I think I've heard enough," the dean says. "We'll email you with our decision."

"Right." I force a brittle smile. "Thank you for your time."

"Thank you, Ms. Burke." He gives me one last smile, then the meetings ends, kicking me out. My smile holds for a moment before it breaks. I ran away from home for that. I missed my dad's death anniversary for that. Everything I've done, and I won't even be able to make my dad proud.

I drop my head in my hands and finally let myself cry.

After my meeting, I change into a pair of Aisling's workout leggings and a long-sleeved shirt in between meals and curl up in a ball on my side of the bed, sleeves wrapped around my fingers so tightly they turn white.

Florence comes in a little after. I hear the door open, but I don't turn around.

"Brennan just found me," she says after a few moments.

I shrug. "Sorry I'm not being very princess-y today." Between the meeting and the anniversary of my father's death, I haven't left the room.

"The first year is always the hardest."

I turn around at that and sit up. "You've…" I trail off. How am I supposed to end that sentence?

"Both of my parents died in a car accident when I was twenty-one," she tells me.

"Well, now I feel like shit," I say. "Or shittier, I guess."

Florence cocks her head. "What do you mean?"

"I just lost my dad. You lost both of them."

"I bet you lost your mom in a way, too, though."

"It's not the same."

"Don't do that," Florence says gently. She moves closer and reaches a hand out but lets it drop before she touches me.

"Do what?" I ask.

"Trivialize your grief."

More tears leak from my eyes. I angrily scrub them away.

"No one's grief is the same. And sometimes, it hits differently. Most of the time, I'm fine, but sometimes, it will hit me out of nowhere, and I have to just deal with it." Florence sits on the edge of the bed near my feet. Her back is straight, but she looks down at her folded hands in her lap. "You don't really get days off when you're in charge of the heir to the throne."

"What?" I would've thought that working with the royal family came with many, many perks. Florence seems to read that on my face.

"It's not bad work, and I love Aisling like my little sister. I can take sick days, and I get a week for vacation, but oftentimes, I can't take them because of some emergency. I try to plan for the anniversary of their deaths, but even that isn't guaranteed."

"Does Aisling know?"

"Yes, but Aisling can only do so much. If the king or queen needs me to do something for her, I have to do it," Florence says.

"But how do you do it?" I ask. "How do you go on, pretending like everything is fine?"

"You can't stop living because they did, Chava," Florence says softly. She puts her hand on my knee, pats it once, and then gets up from the bed. "I'll come check on you later, when they bring up dinner."

She leaves as quietly as she came in. I flop back down against the pillows, my hair extensions flying up around my face. I fight the urge to grab them and yank, irritated at how they get in my way. It may not be my real hair, but it is attached to it. It would still hurt.

I roll off the bed and get to my feet. Walking into Aisling's closet, I pick the first pair of non-heeled shoes I can find and slip them on. Then, I grab a hair tie from her vanity and pull my hair up into a ponytail, something I haven't done in a year. The pulling at my temples feels strange. I can't wait until my hair only hits my chin again.

I walk over to the bedroom door and slowly open it. Peeking my head out, I see no one. Cautiously, I step out and shut the door behind me. I hadn't gotten a chance to see the palace, really see it, and I needed to get out of that room.

Maybe this had been a bad idea. I'd done it to help out Aisling, and myself, but I'd hoped that having space would make me feel better. Instead, I just feel guilt. Guilt in abandoning my family, even if my mother didn't know it, even if we'd been fighting more recently. The guilt had only increased with the knowledge that Aaron knew I was gone, too.

It was all too much. It was eating me alive.

I began walking down the hallway, keeping close to the edge. Even though I'm masquerading as the princess, I'm still nervous soldiers will leap out at any moment and demand to know who I am and why I'm in the palace.

The wall I walk beside is full of grand windows, with gold-gilded edges. I let my hand trail along the sill and check my fingertips. No dust.

Impressive.

Everything about the palace is impressive, to be honest. The walls are a pale gray, and the floors are carpeted in a darker shade. Chandeliers hang from the ceiling every few feet, as if anyone needs a reminder they're in a palace.

I catch a glimpse of a garden through one of the large windows. I turn around, intent on finding the door that leads out there, and jump when I see Brennan standing a few feet behind me.

"Hi," he says.

"Were you following me?" I ask.

He doesn't answer. Instead, he squints at my face and steps closer. "Are you crying?"

I bring my hand to my face, checking to see if my cheeks are wet. They're still damp and a little itchy.

"No," I lie.

Brennan frowns. "What's wrong?"

"Nothing! It's just—it's just a bad day." I fold my arms across my chest and stare down at my feet, not wanting to see Brennan's face. I don't know how to explain my tears to him; I don't know what excuse to give as Aisling, and I don't have the energy to try.

"Well, I have to go to my tuxedo fitting," Brennan says. I nod, still not looking up. "But if you're still feeling bad later, you should meet me in the kitchens tonight. I have a trick for when I'm feeling sad."

At that, I do look up. "What?"

"Ten o'clock, okay?" Brennan doesn't wait for me to answer, already jogging backward.

"I never agreed," I call after him.

"Trust me!" he says, and then he's around the corner.

# CHAPTER FIFTEEN
# AISLING

EMILIA STANDS ON THE STEPS that lead up to the building where the fundraiser is being held when we arrive. She wears the suit she'd picked out yesterday and the silvery top she'd mentioned. Her hair is piled on top of her head in an elegant bun, though a few bubblegum pink strands frame her face. She slouches just so, hands in her pockets, but she straightens up when she sees me.

"Chava!" Emilia smiles brightly, white teeth sparkling. She takes a few strides toward me so that we meet in the middle. Before I can say anything, she throws her arms around me and pulls me into her. My chin lands on her shoulder, and my nose fills with the scent of lavender. Far too soon, she pulls back, her smile dimmed.

"How are you doing today?" she asks.

"Fine," I say, a little dazed.

Emilia's brow furrows. "Fine?"

Aaron coughs loudly and obnoxiously behind me. Oh, right. *Today.*

"I mean," I say, rearranging my face to an expression that I hope seems sad, "as fine as I can be."

Emilia nods sadly. She turns to Melissa then and gathers her in a hug as well. I glance back at Aaron who makes a face at me. I shrug helplessly. I'm a princess, not an actress.

Melissa lets go of Emilia and turns to me with a somewhat forced smile.

"Are you ready to go in?" she asks.

"I guess," Aaron says.

Melissa turns to me, eyebrow quirked in question.

"I'm ready, Mama," I say.

Gian puts his arm around Melissa, and she practically melts into his embrace. She smiles at her father and claps her hands together once, as if to say *Let's go!* and heads to the entrance. Emilia takes a step closer to me, watching Melissa's form disappear up the stairs and into the building.

"Your mom seems kind of… fragile," she says.

"Fragile?" I ask.

Emilia gives me an unimpressed look. "Come on, Chava. Think about how hard this day is for you. You too, Aaron. Now, imagine dealing with that on top of raising two kids alone, not to mention having to act like everything is okay for those two kids. I'm beyond impressed that she put together this fundraiser. Hell, I'm impressed she's not curled up in a ball on her bed in her pajamas."

I hadn't thought about it like that. I had recognized that Melissa was probably just as sad as Chava, but I had assumed she was doing this because she wanted to. Now, I wondered if it was less of a want and more of a need, like a shark—keep moving forward, and you won't die. How strong were the seams that were holding Melissa together? Were they about to come apart?

I thought back to the days when Florence would be a little less put together. She'd never told me what day her parents had died, probably so I wouldn't feel as much guilt if she had to work on the anniversary. But I still felt guilty, and I still saw through the nonchalant facade she put up.

Melissa was like that now, I realize.

"I hadn't thought about it," I say.

"Listen, I know what I said when we broke up was cruel," Emilia says. What did she say to Chava when they broke up? "But there was some truth to it. You know that. You're so wrapped up in your own grief you can't see what's happening in front of you. With your mom, and with Aaron."

I blink, trying desperately to figure out what was said between them. Being wrapped up in my own grief? Maybe that worked for Chava, but what about for me, for Aisling? I wasn't grieving, but maybe I was being selfish. This whole week was a chance for me to be selfish, but that didn't mean I couldn't ease the burden on Chava's family.

Emilia sighs and puts a hand on my shoulder. "I'm going inside. I'll meet you in there." She walks away before I can say anything. I'm confused—what had I done to make her leave me?

I turn to Aaron helplessly.

"I think she wanted to give us space," he says, wrapping his arms around himself.

"To do what?" I ask.

"To talk," he says, "about feelings."

"Do you want to talk about feelings?" I haven't known Aaron long, but he doesn't seem like the type to wear his heart on his sleeve.

Aaron sighs. "Not with you."

My mind is churning, trying to keep up with all the information being thrown at me. Melissa is secretly falling apart. Emilia is upset or disappointed or something I can't quite figure out. And Aaron...

He turns and walks inside the fundraiser before I can say anything else.

After an hour of walking around the fundraiser, people holding my hands and telling me how sorry they are for my loss, I understand why Chava was so desperate to avoid this. It's annoying to me, but I can't imagine how it would feel to her. Annoyed, probably. Sad, definitely. Barely holding it together, like Melissa. I glance over to where Chava's mom stands with Gian and some other people. There's a woman beside her who has a hand on her shoulder, nodding sympathetically. Melissa wears a soft smile, but I can see the glassy look in her eye. She wants to ditch, probably as much as Chava did.

Aaron disappeared about fifteen minutes into the party, a book in his hand. I wouldn't be surprised if he was hiding under a table somewhere or off in some empty room. I wish I could join him.

The only saving grace to this fundraiser is Emilia. She stands close by my side the entire time and steps in when people tend to get into more personal territory regarding Chava's dad. I know she's doing it to keep "Chava" from getting upset, but it works out for me—I don't know childhood stories or inside jokes or favorite memories or anything people ask about. I'd been so busy preparing Chava to be me that I hadn't considered learning more than the basics about her.

Was that selfish of me, too? Had I decided my life was so much more important than hers, subconsciously?

Emilia shoves a napkin into my hand, breaking me out of my thoughts. I look down to see a mini cupcake, chocolate with white frosting and a slice of strawberry on top.

"I got your favorite," she tells me with a small smile. "It was nice of your mom to get your guys' favorite food."

I cock my head questioningly.

Emilia laughs. "She's got mini pigs in a blanket for Aaron and your favorite dessert."

"Oh." I shove the cupcake in my mouth so that I don't have to say anything else. It's probably the most unladylike thing that I've ever done in my entire life, and a little thrill rushes through me at the thought. Another thrill rushes through me as Emilia laughs, this time at my antics.

"You've got chocolate on your face," she says. Before I can react, she brings her thumb up to the corner of my mouth and wipes it away. I shiver as the pad of her thumb brushes against the sensitive skin of my lip, even if it is just the corner. My eyes close of their own accord, but I quickly force them open. When I do, I see Emilia staring at me, something soft in her gaze.

"Got it," she whispers, dropping her hand to her side.

Melissa appears beside us, and I jump, too caught up in the moment. Had I just had that moment with Emilia? Or had I imagined it? There's no way she would look at someone she'd just broken up with like that, even if they were still friends. Exes didn't look at each other like that. I *was* imagining things.

"Chava, it's time for the speech," Melissa tells me. I fight the urge to physically shake my head, to rid myself of these intrusive and unwanted thoughts. I'm reading too far into things and making mountains out of molehills. Melissa's words register.

"Speech?" I have to give a speech? My heart stops.

"Yes, my speech. I want you and Aaron to stand up there with me. Where is your brother?" Melissa looks around, which gives me time to recover from the heart attack she'd just given me. I just have to stand up there and look pretty. Or maybe solemn? Either way, it's something I have plenty of practice with—being an ornament.

"I don't know," I say in answer to her question.

"Doesn't Aaron have stage fright?" Emilia asks.

"He won't have to do anything," Melissa assures her. "Now, have you seen him?"

"He was getting some food a minute ago," Emilia says.

The three of us turn to the food table. Aaron leans against the wall behind it, a pig in a blanket in one hand and his book in the other. Melissa heads over there, with an order over her shoulder for me to make my way to the stage.

"Well, I guess I should go up there," I say, a little awkwardly. I was way into her hand on my face, though I'm loath to admit it. I hate to think that I've ruined the relationship Chava and Emilia had built back up after their breakup.

"Have fun," Emilia teases, eyes bright. I let out a silent breath of relief. Nothing seems amiss. I smile back before squeezing my way through the crowds and up the few stairs to the small stage at the front of the room. Melissa follows a moment later with Aaron skulking behind her.

A low buzzing noise starts up, and I turn to see that a screen is being lowered on the wall. It clicks into place, and then a picture is blown up. It's of the man I've seen in Chava's pictures, his wide smile front and center.

I turn back to see Melissa and Aaron frozen, staring at the picture transfixed. Tears well in Melissa's eyes and overflow. Her hand comes up to cover her mouth. I take a step forward, so that I'm closer to her.

"Mama? Are you okay?" I ask.

Melissa nods shakily. She clears her throat and straightens up, wiping her eyes. She goes up to the podium and taps on the microphone, the feedback echoing throughout the room. The murmur of conversation comes to a halt, and everyone turns to stare at us.

Beside me, I feel Aaron stiffen. I put my arm around his shoulders and pull him closer, angled so that he's standing slightly behind me. He relaxes momentarily but reaches up to squeeze my hand on his shoulder. I glance down at him.

*Thank you*, he mouths. I smile in answer.

"Welcome." Melissa's voice booms around the room, drawing our attention back to her. "I'd like to thank you all for coming here today in support of finding a cure for brain cancer. As some of you may know, last year, I lost my husband to brain cancer. A year ago today, exactly. My kids lost their father." Melissa's voice breaks. Her hand flies up to her throat, which she rubs anxiously. "I—I'm sorry. Um, I'm here today to tell you about his story. Adam's story. My husband's name was Adam. Um, two and a half years ago, Adam began to have seizures. He, um, he went to the hospital to get a CAT scan done. We'd just hoped—God, I don't know what we'd hoped. Anything other than the answer that we got. And it was—it's just—" Melissa chokes on a sob. She buries her face in her hands. "I'm sorry. I'm sorry. I'm so sorry."

I stand there, shocked and unsure of what to do. Aaron stands beside me, unmoving. Emilia said he had stage fright. He won't be able to do anything.

And as the oldest child, Chava should be the one to do something, shouldn't she? Shouldn't I?

Mind made up, I walk up to Melissa and pull her into a hug. She buries her head in my shoulder and takes gasping breaths.

"It's okay, Mama," I say soothingly, patting her back. "I've got this." I pass Melissa off to Aaron, who willingly steps into his mother's embrace. Melissa manages to get a semblance of control and straightens up, though tears still flow freely down her face. I take a deep breath and turn to face the audience.

"Hi," I say awkwardly. I've been groomed all my life to give public speeches, but I've never done one in front of so many people before. It's always been small groups, like Parliament, and they've always been pre-written. And I've always been the heir to the throne, Princess Aisling. Now, I'm a normal girl. Chava Burke. A girl who lost her father.

What do I say?

"You've probably figured this out by now," I say into the microphone, "but I'm her child." There are muffled chuckles from the crowd, as if they don't know whether they should laugh or not.

"My name is Chava, and Adam Burke was my dad." Stick to facts, Aisling, stuff that people can't poke holes in. "I was fifteen when my dad was diagnosed with cancer, old enough to understand what was happening but not old enough for it to be fair. But I mean, when is cancer ever fair? When is life ever fair?"

I look back over my shoulder at Aaron and Melissa. Aaron still has a slight deer-in-headlights look, but he nods at me when I catch his eye. I take a deep breath and turn back to the room.

"I've struggled to find a place in this world, especially after my father was diagnosed. Growing up, I expected one thing, but suddenly, that one thing was turned upside down. My life, my future—everything changed. Instead of choices, I had expectations. I couldn't be the person I wanted to be, but part of me… part of me didn't even know who that was. It was all cut off. I never got the chance to try.

"I don't know who I want to be, exactly, but I know I want to be someone my father would be proud of. A loving daughter and sister, a good friend, and... and someone who takes risks. Because cancer—cancer doesn't care if you've taken risks in your life or not. It doesn't care if you've eaten healthy every day or if you've gone skydiving. It chooses you anyway.

"I don't want to live my life afraid of what could happen because there was nothing that could have been done to stop my father from getting brain cancer, so what is there to stop me from getting it? And if one day, I end up in a hospital bed, I don't want to spend the last few days or hours or minutes of my life regretting what I could have done. And my father wouldn't have wanted that for me either.

"I don't know if this was the speech you were expecting," I continue. The audience laughs. I look back at Melissa and Aaron once more. Melissa steps forward, dragging Aaron behind her, and grabs my hand. "I didn't have a lot of time to prepare it. But we're here today to raise money for brain cancer awareness and to remember my father. And the best way I can remember my father is by living a life he would be proud of. Thank you."

As much as I love dressing up in pretty dresses, it is a relief to slip into Chava's well-worn pajamas when we get home. I sit on the blue bedspread, staring at the pattern of puppies in funny hats on the pajama pants and picking at a loose thread on the knee. My mind races as I replay the impromptu speech that I'd given. Had it been good enough? Had I acted and spoken enough like Chava? Had Emilia or Melissa expected anything?

There's a knock on my door, and I look up.

"Come in," I say.

The door creaks open, revealing Melissa standing in the doorway. She's changed out of her fundraiser clothes as well, into an old purple Purdue sweatshirt and gray sweatpants. Her black hair is pulled back away from her face in a ponytail. I'm struck with both how old and young she looks at the same time. Old, in the sense that she's experienced so much, and young, in the hesitation on her face.

She takes a few halting steps in and stops at the foot of the bed, motioning down toward it. "Can I sit?"

I nod, and she does, perching on the edge. Melissa doesn't quite look at me, instead staring at the bedside table that boasts a picture of a young Chava on her dad's shoulders, both of their faces lit up with joy. A faint smile graces Melissa's face.

"You were great up there tonight, sweetheart," she says.

I'm a little shocked at the endearment. We don't use those at the palace, always referred to by name or by title. And I haven't heard Melissa say anything but Chava or Aaron's names in the few days I've been here.

"I know you didn't want to go tonight," Melissa continues before I can stammer out a response, "and I'm sure you didn't want to give that speech. I didn't want to give that speech, and I'd been planning it for weeks. I even memorized it, for as much good as that did me."

Melissa sighs. "I always forget how strong you are, Chava. I don't know why. I see it time and time again. Every time you don't back down from a fight. Every time you rise to the challenge. Every time you grin and bear it, and I know you've done that a lot in the last few years."

"I know—" She takes a deep breath and closes her eyes. "I know I haven't been the best mom over the past year. I haven't been there for you like I should have been.

I've been so focused on making your father's death mean something that I haven't stopped to focus on the best thing your dad could have left behind—you and Aaron."

Melissa turns on the bed and grabs my hand, gripping it tightly. Her eyes are bright with unshed tears, and when she speaks, her voice is thick. I feel paralyzed. I don't know what to do; I shouldn't be the one hearing this.

"I love you, Chava, so much. You and Aaron both. I don't know if I've said that enough, but I should have. I should have said it every day, because if losing your father taught me anything, it's that nothing is promised. One day you can be here, and the next you can be gone. From now on, I'm going to do better. I'm going to *be* better," she promises fiercely.

Unbidden, tears rise to my eyes as well. My mother has never been this passionate about anything, let alone about me. Again, I'm struck with the fact that if my mom knew I was gay, I don't know what she would do. I don't know if she would still love me.

But this woman in front of me, she does love her daughter, no matter what. And now, here she is, swearing to be the kind of mom a daughter needs.

Would my mom do that?

"I love you, too, Mama," I say, barely able to speak past the tears.

Melissa pulls me into a tight hug. I wrap my arms around her. We say nothing for a few minutes, simply holding each other on the blue bedspread.

Finally, I let go, pulling back to wipe at my eyes.

"Have you said this to Aaron?" I ask.

Melissa laughs a little, though it sounds more like a croak. "I don't know if he would let me. You know how he gets with acts of affection. But I am going to tell him that I love him more than life itself."

"I think he'd like that," I say. "Sometimes, it's just nice to hear."

Melissa gives me one last smile and a kiss on the head and leaves the room. Finally alone, I breathe a sigh of relief. I grab Chava's phone from where I'd left it on the nightstand.

There are several notifications from the dating app, and I click on them. More people have reached out to me, but Hallie's conversation is still at the top.

I click on the conversation.

**Me:** Hey!

**Hallie:** I know this is last minute, but do you have plans tomorrow night?

It was sent nearly an hour ago. I scramble to respond that no, I don't have plans tomorrow. Three little dots appear, signaling her typing.

**Hallie:** Cool! Would you wanna go to that new club with me? The Ephemeral Bar on Main?

I have no idea what that is, but I respond enthusiastically. She responds with a time—ten o'clock—to which I agree. She texts again, asking me what I do for a living, but I'm too high on cloud nine to respond right away.

A date. I actually have a date. I *finally* have a date.

And if all goes well, I'm going to kiss a girl.

# CHAPTER SIXTEEN
## CHAVA

I MEET BRENNAN IN THE KITCHENS later that night. They're empty and dark, and I'm taken aback by all the stainless steel. Brennan stands in the middle of the tiled floor, the flashlight from his phone lighting him up in a fluorescent halo. He grins when he sees me.

"You came," he says happily.

"You said you had a trick for when you were sad," I say, walking closer. "I was curious."

"Well, then, you came to the right person." Brennan sets his phone down on the nearest counter, the light seeping through the room.

"So, what are we doing in the kitchens?" I ask.

"Baking," Brennan tells me, walking over to the gigantic fridge and opening the doors wide. My eyes pop out of my head as he surveys the options.

"Dukes bake?" I ask incredulously. Don't they have people to do that for them?

"Do princesses?" he returns.

I shake my head. "Not this one." I don't know if Aisling bakes or not—I'd imagine not, just going off her sheltered personality—but I certainly do not. We are not a family of bakers. Our brownies for bake sales in elementary school always came from the nearest supermarket.

"I guess I'll have to teach you," Brennan says, glancing at me over his shoulder. He smiles a smile that pulls across his face, his teeth straight and even and perfectly white, then turns back to the contents of the fridge. He pulls out a carton of eggs and a stick of butter and places them on the counter. "You don't happen to know where the baking goods are? Flour, sugar, stuff like that?"

"Is there a pantry somewhere?" I ask.

"Help me look," Brennan says. I sigh but join him in searching for the pantry. I can't imagine there are many options for where a large closet with extra food would be hiding, but it's dark and hard to see. Unlike Brennan, I didn't bring my phone.

I feel along the wall on the opposite side from where Brennan is scanning his flashlight. My hand catches on a handle, and I pull it open. Automatic lights flip on, revealing shelves full of baking items, pasta, rice, and more. But it's not a pantry—it's its own separate room, bigger than my bedroom.

"Uh, Brennan?" I say. "I found it."

Brennan jogs over, phone in hand, and pauses beside me. "Wow. This is like a chef's paradise."

"So, yours?" I ask. Brennan laughs as he steps farther inside, heading over to the section full of bags of flour and brown sugar.

"Not quite," he says. "I'm not a chef. But my dad… he kind of was. More of a baker, really. That's how I learned to bake. We'd make something at least once a week—cookies, brownies, cupcakes, you name it—and then we'd deliver it to the orphanages or the women's shelter or the people working in our home. We switched it up."

Brennan sighs. "When he died, I—I kind of fell out of it for a while. But then my sisters wanted Dad's famous chocolate chip cookies for a sleepover one night, and they insisted that I was the only one who could make them like him. I don't really agree, but it got me back into it. And while I was baking… it was like he was there with me."

Brennan turns back to me, arms loaded up with baking supplies.

"I'm sorry. You're feeling sad today, and here I am, bringing the mood down." Brennan gives me a somewhat bitter smile.

"No, it's okay," I assure him. "I like hearing about your dad. It makes me think of mine."

"How?"

"It just… what you said, about feeling like he was there. I get that. Or, I wish I got that. I haven't felt like my dad was with me in a long time."

"I take it you don't have a close relationship with the king?"

It's like a bucket of ice cold water to the face. I'm Aisling right now, not Chava. We're not bonding over our dead fathers. The only person in this room whose father is dead is Brennan, not me.

I take a sharp breath and let it out. "Oh, uh, not really. But I mean, what can you expect when your dad's the king, right?"

"Aisling—"

Her name burns.

"So are you going to teach me how to bake or what?" I ask, smiling. I can only hope it doesn't look as brittle as it feels.

When I get back to the room, a plate of warm cookies in hand, it's past eleven. I wince a little when I see the time, though. That's going to suck when I have to wake up at 6:30 the next morning. I set the plate on the bedside table and throw myself down on the bed. As I grab Aisling's phone, I grab a cookie as well and shove it in my mouth.

I chew slowly, savoring it, letting the chocolate melt against my tongue. The duke's famous chocolate chip cookies certainly deserve their moniker.

I open up Aisling's contacts and hover over my name, wondering if the fundraiser is over yet. Before I can debate it, the phone rings with an incoming call from "Chava." I answer it and hold the phone up to my ear.

"Hello?"

"Hey, it's me." Aisling's voice filters over the phone, sounding a little strained.

"Hey, how did tonight go?" I ask.

"I think it went well," Aisling says. "I had to give a speech for your mom, though."

My stomach drops. "No."

"It's fine," she assures me. "I pulled something out of thin air, and everyone seemed to like it. Your mom seemed to believe it, and she's the main one to impress, right?"

"I guess," I say uncertainly. I shudder a little at the thought of it having been me up there tonight, having to give a speech. That would have been the cherry on top of an already awful sundae.

"Hey, so, uh, speaking of your mom," Aisling says. She pauses.

"Yeah?" I prompt.

"I know that you've been having a hard time with her, and I totally get that. Well, I mean, I don't like 'get it' get it because I don't get in arguments with my mom, but I guess I understand you're having a hard time with your mom, and I'm totally sympathetic to that."

"Okay…"

"But it's just… I think your mom is having a really hard time, too."

"No one is saying she isn't," I say. "But you don't know what it's been like with her since my dad died. She's so concerned about appearances and this stupid fundraiser and—"

"But have you considered that she was only so focused on those things so that she didn't have to think about other things?" Aisling asks.

"You mean, like her children?" I demand.

"What? No, of course not—"

"Because that's what it's felt like," I say. "Aisling, I appreciate you going to the fundraiser for me, I really do, but I don't need you coming into my life for a couple of days and suddenly deciding you understand my mother better than I do. You haven't lived with her for the past year. You haven't had to be perfect and hide away your grief and move to an entire fucking different country. You haven't lost your dad. So maybe don't try to tell me things about my mother and my family and my life."

I hang up the phone before Aisling can answer and throw it across the room.

# CHAPTER SEVENTEEN
# AISLING

Melissa is called into work that morning, and Gian has left for a bridge game already, so Aaron doesn't have a ride to his science fair. We stand at the kitchen table, looking at his volcano thoughtfully.

"We could carry it together?" I offer.

Aaron makes a face. "What if someone runs into us?"

"Well, we don't have a car, and even if we did, I can't drive," I say.

Aaron sighs. "I can't believe Mama forgot. She would've left the car if she remembered."

I place a hand on his shoulder. "She's trying."

"I know." He frowns. "That doesn't make the things she fails at any easier."

"Can one of your friends' parents take us?" I ask.

"No," Aaron says, raising a finger, "but one of *your* friends can."

"I don't have friends."

"One of Chava's friends."

"Chava doesn't seem to really have friends, either."

"Just call Emilia!"

I blink. "Emilia has a car?"

"Her family does," Aaron says, "but I'm sure she can borrow it to take me to the science fair. Come on, call her, it starts in less than an hour."

I do as he says, and Emilia assures me she'll be there in fifteen minutes. She makes it in ten, and Aaron and I carefully take the volcano from the table to the backseat of the car, where he climbs in beside it and puts his arm protectively around it.

"Drive," he orders.

Emilia shoots him a look. He withers.

"Please," he adds.

"Better," she says. She pulls the car out onto the street and heads in a direction I've yet to take. I look outside the window as we pass through a different side of town, smaller houses and even smaller shops. Eventually, we pull up to the school, a big brick building with large glass windows and the words *The International School of Vyctorya* attached to the front.

Emilia sighs as Aaron gets out of the car. "Didn't think I'd have to come back here."

I shrug, unsure of what to say, and get out to help Aaron carry his volcano. Emilia walks ahead of us, holding doors open. Finally, we manage to get to the gymnasium where the science fair is being held. Aaron checks in, and the guide tells him his table number. Then, Aaron and I are carefully making our way to his table and laying it on top. And it's done. Aaron's science project made it to his science fair safe and sound.

"It looks great, Aaron," Emilia says, watching us.

"Thanks," Aaron says. He reaches into his backpack and pulls out several laminated pages and lays them out, talking all about volcanoes. I look around at the other kids with their projects—some with just posters, others with trifolds, and some with their physical projects.

"What time does it start?" I ask.

"Ten o'clock," Aaron says. "It goes til two, and the awards ceremony is at two-thirty."

"Like first, second, and third?" I ask.

Aaron shrugs. "Yeah, basically.

"It's almost ten now," Emilia says. "Do you need help setting up?"

"No, but I do need you two to go away," Aaron says, gaze trained beyond us. "The judges are looking around, and you're in the way."

"Okay, we'll go stand in someone else's way," Emilia says, grabbing my arm and pulling me off. She's giggling slightly, shaking her head fondly. "Aaron is so funny."

"Yeah," I agree. "He can be very serious."

"So serious!" Emilia says. "It's adorable."

"I think he'd punch you if he heard you say that," I tell her. That sends her into another fit of giggles, ones that start me laughing too. Emilia has a beautiful, infectious laugh.

Once our laughter quiets down, I look around the science fair. It's about to start, students getting ready to start their spiels as people come up to their booths.

"Do you want to walk around?" I ask. "Check out the competition?"

Emilia's face lights up for a moment, but it falls just as quickly. She sighs, looking at the floor.

"I can't. I have to get back to the café."

"You were scheduled today?" I'm a little horrified that Aaron and I called her away.

"No, no, not really," she assures me. "My mom said it was fine for me to come pick you guys up. But… we had to lay off some of our employees, so now we're short staffed, and I have to fill in the gaps."

The words she says swim around in my head for a bit— *lay off? Short staffed?*

"Is everything okay?" I ask.

"Yeah, it's all good," Emilia says. "But I do have to get going. What time does this thing end again? Three? I can pick you up, if you need."

"I'll check with Gi—Dada and see if he can pick us up. I'd hate for you to miss more work," I say, feeling immensely guilty. Emilia seems nervous about being away from the cafe, picking at her nails and worrying her lip. But she smiles at me anyway and touches my arm.

"If you're sure," she says, "but let me know if he can't, okay?"

"Okay," I tell her. "And let me know if Aaron wins!" she adds as she starts to walk away, still facing me.

"I will!"

"Bye, Chava!"

"Bye," I whisper, waving a hand, but she's already turned around, heading for the double doors of the gymnasium.

# CHAPTER EIGHTEEN
# CHAVA

The next morning, my eyes feel puffy and swollen. After I'd thrown Aisling's phone, I'd buried my head in her stupid down-filled pillow and cried myself to sleep. Florence glares at me as I apply eye cream to the bags under my eyes.

"This does not look very princess-y," she informs me.

I huff. "Newsflash: I'm not a princess!"

"Shh!" Florence glances around Aisling's room, as if we aren't the only two people here. I roll my eyes as I grab the eyeshadow I'm expected to put on.

"What, is the room bugged? I didn't realize the Royal Family employed the CIA."

"What is up with you this morning? Even yesterday, you weren't this crabby," Florence says, crossing her arms over her chest. I feel my blood start to boil.

"You don't know me. Maybe this is how I am every day," I say, stabbing the eyeshadow brush into the powder.

Florence grabs the palette from me and sets it back on the vanity, then grabs my shoulder and turns me to face her.

"What is wrong with you?" she asks slowly. Her face is open, encouraging, like she really wants to know what's wrong. But she's here for Aisling, not for me.

"Nothing!" I say, voice breaking on the second syllable. My anger is feral, like a wild dog, biting at my heels. I want the hurt. I want to make others hurt.

Florence's face closes off. She lets go of me and straightens up. "Fine, then. Finish getting ready and meet me outside before we go to breakfast. Your outfit is in the closet. Gracelynn is coming to the palace today for your final dress fitting."

That sends me for a loop.

"Gracelynn is coming here?" I demand.

Florence's eyes widen. "Is that a problem?"

"I can't keep this up in front of her! She'll see right through me!"

"What? Why?"

"She's my godmother! We used to FaceTime every week! We have dinner together every Sunday!"

"I'm sorry. You think that Aisling can fool your mom into believing she's you, but you can't fool Gracelynn into believing you're Aisling?" Florence raises an eyebrow.

"My mom's been busy. She barely pays attention to me anymore. But Gracelynn—" I cut myself off, unsure what else to say.

"You have to do this," Florence says. "We need a final fitting. There's no time before the wedding."

"What do we do when Gracelynn finds out?" I ask.

"She won't," Florence says firmly.

"But—"

"She won't. Aisling never talks much; that's usually my job. I'll be there the entire time, running interference. It will be fine," Florence says.

"But—"

"It'll be fine."

"But what if—"

"Fine!"

"Fine!" I huff and turn back to the mirror, grabbing the palette and stabbing at it once more. Florence sighs as she watches me. I almost don't hear her mutter to herself, "It'll be fine."

But I do.

A plain blue sundress with a crocheted white cardigan is easy enough to slip off behind the privacy partition. I wrap my arms around my bare midriff, standing in the matching blue underwear as there is shuffling on the other side of the room.

Apparently, I have to try the wedding dress on in the bridal room, where the bride gets ready for the wedding. Florence says it's tradition. I'm really beginning to hate tradition.

The room is white with hints of pink roses everywhere. There are breezy, lace white curtains dangling from the tall windows letting the sunshine through, creating dazzling patterns on the hardwood floor. There are antique lounging couches and overstuffed chairs and ottomans placed around the room.

"Where's the princess?" Gracelynn's voice floats over the partition, and I tense up, even though she can't see me. For a panicked moment, I worry she has X-Ray vision, or maybe mind reading powers, and she's about to uncover all of my secrets.

"She's waiting behind the partition," Florence says. "She's eager to try on the gown."

"Eager?" Doubt colors Gracelynn's tone. "She didn't really seem eager last time she was trying it on."

"She's met the duke since then, and they've really hit it off," Florence tells her.

"Really? That's wonderful. I'm so happy for them. You know, when I was first commissioned for this dress, I was worried Her Highness was sort of being strong-armed into this, but it makes me feel so much better to know she's getting along with the duke." As Gracelynn talks, my stomach twists further and further. I can't tell whether it's because Aisling doesn't really know the duke and that they might actually have a terrible marriage… or if it's the fact that Aisling will be the one married to Brennan.

I nearly smack myself at that thought. What, as if *I* should be the one to marry Brennan? No way in hell. I'm eighteen, and I just met the guy.

*What are you thinking, Chava?* I ask myself.

"Oh, by the way, this is my assistant, Melissa. She's come to help with the fitting."

I freeze. Melissa. My *mother*.

"Let me take the dress," Florence says. Is it just me, or does she finally sound nervous?

"Oh, usually, I help the bride into it…"

"Aisling can manage today."

After a moment, Florence appears at the edge of the partition and hangs the dress on the hook, shooting me a warning look, before vanishing once more. I hear her voice mingling with Gracelynn's as I take a hesitant step toward the garment bag that holds the dress.

I unzip the bag slowly, my hands shaking a little. Inch by inch, white silk appears overlaid in lace and tiny pearlescent beads. The full skirt flops out of the bag when the zipper reaches the floor and blows gently in the breeze created by the air conditioning. Looking at the dress, I'm not so sure I can easily step into it anymore.

Nevertheless, I take it off the hanger and pull it out of the bag. The back of the dress is a line of buttons, but they're all luckily undone, so it really is just a matter of stepping in and finding my footing through the yards of fabric that make up the underskirt. I pull the silk up over my hips and to my chest, sliding my arms through the long, lace sleeves.

I clutch the bodice to my chest to keep it up as I step out from behind the partition. Gracelynn stops talking, bringing her hands to her mouth when she sees me.

"Oh, Your Highness, you look just like a princess," she says, "which is good because you are one." She giggles at her own joke then motions me closer. Beside her, my mother stands, her eyes wide.

"Oh my God," Mama says.

"Is everything okay?" Florence asks, stepping in front of me slightly.

"I'm sorry," Gracelynn says. "This is going to sound so weird. But the princess looks a lot like Melissa's daughter. It's uncanny really. I warned her up front, but I doubt she believed me."

Mama's mouth is practically on the floor. She looks like she wants to touch me but holds herself back. "You were serious. She looks just like Chava." I fight the urge to wince at the sound of my name, but finally, I take slow steps to Gracelynn, not wanting to get too close. She turns me around as soon as I'm within arms' reach and begins doing up the buttons on my back.

"How does it feel?" Gracelynn asks, hands fluttering around my lower back.

Florence steps out in front of me and surveys the dress with a critical eye. She nods to herself and gives me a small smile.

"Beautiful," I say honestly. I doubt that I'll ever wear something as beautiful again in my entire life, even my own wedding dress, if I should ever get married. And it's certainly the most expensive thing, I'm positive of that. I think the pearlescent beads are actual pearls.

"Some of my finest work, if I do say so myself," Gracelynn says, halfway up my back now.

My stomach begins to churn uncomfortably. After she's done with my back, then she'll have to get up close and personal, checking to make sure everything fits right and that there are no loose threads or anything. That is when my secret will be at its most vulnerable. I'm not ready for that moment.

"And done," Gracelynn says. I feel her take a step back and practically see her nod. "Those buttons are a piece of work, but they really add something to the dress."

"It's perfect, Gracelynn," Florence says.

"It will be, once I add the finishing touches," Gracelynn says, coming around so she stands in front of me. Mama shuffles behind, still a little awestruck, but ready with a measuring tape and a notebook.

I automatically stiffen, then work to drop my shoulders. Gracelynn is too busy examining the dress to notice.

"What finishing touches?" I ask. From what I can tell, everything seems finished and polished to perfection.

"Little nips and tucks to make sure the dress fits you like a glove," she says, moving closer. She holds my arm straight out and begins pulling at the fabric. "A dainty, little kid glove." The last bit is said to herself, in a sing-song-y sort of voice.

I'm a little nervous about that news. Aisling and I are close enough in size, but I don't know if we're exact matches. Nothing seems to be hanging too loosely on me, so I suppose there wouldn't be any major alterations needed, but what if Gracelynn tightens an arm too much and Aisling busts a stitch when she puts it on on Sunday? Or what if it turns out to be too loose and hangs like a bat wing?

"Is that really necessary?" I ask, voice a little higher than it should be.

"You're not going to gain five pounds in the next few days, Your Highness," Gracelynn says, shaking her head as if I'm *just so silly*. "You'll be fine."

"I think it looks perfect as it is, Gracelynn," Florence says. Clearly, she sees the predicament.

"All due respect, my lady, Your Highness, but the king and queen hired me to make the best dress I could make. And there are tiny alterations that will send this dress over the edge—from fashion to history," Gracelynn says, one hand gesturing wildly.

"But—" I cut myself off, unsure of what to argue. I've long known that stopping Gracelynn is no easier than stopping your momentum when you roll down a hill.

"But what, Your Highness?" Gracelynn asks. She's still facing me, but she has her body turned halfway toward Mama, hands outstretched. I shoot a panicked look at Florence; she offers no help.

"What do you think needs adjusting?" I change tactics. I run my hands down the front of the top, smoothing it along my stomach.

"The top is a little loose," Gracelynn says. She motions to the neckline, and I glance down. There is a bit of a gap, maybe an inch, so that I can see down to my chest. I frown.

"Maybe it's the… bra?" I offer.

Gracelynn's eyebrows raise. Florence closes her eyes and winces.

"What?" Gracelynn asks.

"There's just not enough support," I say, trying to thread confidence through my words.

"This dress isn't really meant to be worn with a bra," Gracelynn says.

"Who will be able to tell the difference?"

"Well, no one should, really, but—"

"I would feel more comfortable wearing a bra," I cut in. "More… coverage." I gesture in the general area of my breasts and fight the awkwardness creeping in. I'm a princess right now; princesses can talk about anything they want, right?

Gracelynn seems flabbergasted. She looks at Florence, now perfectly composed, who nods.

"The princess's comfort is our utmost concern," she says firmly.

Gracelynn blinks, turning back to me.

"Well, I suppose you should try the dress on with the correct undergarments then." Gracelynn addresses Florence. "Can we send someone to—"

"I'll go," I blurt. They all three look at me, Gracelynn and Mama with extreme confusion and Florence with incredulousness.

"What—"

I cut off Gracelynn once more.

"I know exactly what I'm looking for," I say. "Anyone else would take forever to search the closet, and I would hate to waste your time. I'm sure your dress shop is very busy."

"Oh, well, I suppose—"

"Great!" I chirp, hopping down from the stool and hurrying through them. Mama watches me, looking like she's seen a ghost. She looks at me like she hasn't seen me in a long time. My eyes burn.

I make for the door without thinking, head down, ignoring Gracelynn's cries of protest. I shove the doors open and walk through them, letting them slam closed behind me. I press my back against the wood for a moment before I push off and dart down the halls, breaths coming in hard and fast, fighting to keep the tears at bay.

I run down the long hallways, taking turns at random and hoping I don't run into anyone. I'm barefoot and in a full ball gown that's just the slightest bit too long, so I have to pick up my skirts like I'm goddamn Cinderella.

As unfamiliar as I am with the castle, this wing is even more confusing. There are fancy doors everywhere, and I have no idea where they lead to. I pause, breathing hard in the middle of the hallway, and check my surroundings.

It dawns on me that I was supposed to go to Aisling's room to look for a bra, but I can't be bothered to deal with that right now. I hear voices at the far end of the hall and panic. No one can see me right now, not in a wedding dress holding back tears.

My eyes catch on the closest door, and I rush over to it, pulling it open and shutting it as quietly as I can behind me.

I slump to the ground, my back against the door, and drop my head into my hands.

Guilt and pain curl in my chest, like a twining weed, choking anything that had life—hope, happiness… maybe even love. Things I had begun to feel when I got to the palace and took over Aisling's life.

Why is Mama looking at the princess like that when she can barely stand to look at me?

I choke on a sob and twist my fingers into my hair, digging at the roots.

I want to scream.

And then there's a hand on my shoulder.

I whip my head up to see Brennan staring at me, clear blue eyes full of concern. He kneels next to me on the floor, posed like he's about to propose. His palm is warm, seeping through the cool silk of the dress.

"Aisling, are you okay?" he asks.

I wipe at my face, hoping to God that no tears had overflowed. My fingers come away dry.

"Yeah, I'm fine," I say.

He gives me an unimpressed look. "You look like you're about to cry… in a wedding dress? Is that your wedding dress?" His eyes widen, and he turns around so fast that he falls down.

"What are you doing?" I ask.

"Isn't it bad luck to see the bride in her dress before the wedding day?" he asks, back still turned to me.

"I don't believe in that," I say.

"I do," he says.

I roll my eyes. "Brennan, it's fine. You've already seen it." And, technically, he hasn't seen the *actual* bride in her dress. Just the dress.

He stands up and walks over to a grand piano that's in the middle of the room. I look around for the first time, taking in the room that I'd rushed into. There are shelves full of thin books and music stands placed around the room. Against the wall, there are a few guitars and black cases of varying sizes.

"What are you doing in here?" I ask. Brennan still doesn't look at me as he slides back onto the bench and presses a key. A crystal-clear note echoes through the room, but he seems dejected somehow, a complete one-eighty from the concerned duke he'd been only moments before.

"Is something wrong?" I ask.

"I don't know," Brennan says, finally twisting on the bench to look at me. "*Is* something wrong? Do you… do you not want to get married to me?"

I blink, stunned.

"Wait, let me rephrase that. I know that getting married probably isn't what you wanted to do, but… it's just—is there a problem with me? Am I making your life worse?" He's always been open, but this is different. He seems so vulnerable, so easy to hurt. Slowly, I walk over and sit down beside him on the bench. I don't look at him, instead staring at the sheet music he's placed on the music stand.

"If I'm being honest with you," I say, "since this week started, you've been the best part." I make sure to choose my words carefully. I can't promise him love, not the romantic kind, because Aisling won't love him that way. But that doesn't mean their life together has to suck.

"I can't promise you something I'm not ready to give, something I may not ever be able to give, but I can promise you that I will be your friend."

Clumsily, I place my right hand on a C Major chord. It chimes merrily throughout the room. "I want us to be like this, to work together, to be happy." I shift my middle finger down to the black key. The minor chord hums through me.

"I don't want to be like this," I say.

"Then why were you upset?" he asks.

I bite my lip, letting my fingers slide off the keys. The light buzz of the music ceases.

"My life is complicated right now," I say honestly. "My head is a jumbled mess, and I don't always know how to deal with it. I tend to run away, which isn't healthy. But right now, I don't know any other options. It's like…" I take a breath. "It's like someone threw me into the deep end of a pool. And I know how to swim, but it's been a while, so I'm struggling. And this probably makes no sense and sounds really dumb."

"No, I get it," Brennan says. "Things are hard. That makes sense. And I'm guessing the dress pushed it over the edge?"

"Something like that," I agree.

The door swings open, revealing Florence. Her eyes widen when she sees me with Brennan.

"Your Grace, what are you doing here?" she asks.

I stand up and walk over to Florence.

"I ran into him, so really, you should be asking me what I'm doing here," I say. "I'm sorry. I'll head back to the bridal room."

Florence nods and, with a pointed look at first Brennan and then me, turns to walk back down the hallway. I make to follow, but Brennan calls my name—Aisling's name—and I pause.

"If you need help swimming," he says, smiling slightly, "just give me a call. I've had a lot of practice in the past few months."

# CHAPTER NINETEEN
# AISLING

I HAVE NO IDEA WHAT TO wear to a club. I've only ever seen clubs on television, and people are usually in slinky outfits showing off more skin than I've ever been allowed to show. I search Chava's closet and finally land on a blue halter-neck crop top and a black skirt. I slip on her tennis shoes and am thankful once again that not only do we look alike, we're the same size.

I find a worn leather shoulder bag and slip the phone and wallet inside. I glance around, wondering if I need anything else for a club, and remember I need to grab Chava's keys so I can get back inside the house when I'm done. I head downstairs, grabbing her keys off the ring, and head for the front door.

I'd asked Melissa for permission to go to the club after dinner, and she'd laughed at me, saying she couldn't remember the last time I'd asked if anything was okay with her. But, nevertheless, she'd agreed and told me to be home by one o'clock at the latest.

Now, I go out the front door and lock it behind me. According to the phone, the club is a twenty-minute walk downtown, so I head out. I could use one of those car service apps, but I don't know how to work them, so walking it is.

Luckily, it's not a difficult walk. I've become somewhat familiar with the turns of the town in the past few days after walking back and forth, and it's well-lit, which is nice. I am a little apprehensive about people mugging or kidnapping me, but I still have my panic button. I reach up and grab where it hangs around my neck just to reassure myself it's still there.

By the time I approach the club, it's nearly ten o'clock, the agreed upon time to meet. Hallie had told me she'd be wearing a rainbow-colored beanie, so I search the crowd as I join the line to get into the club. Around me, people whisper, and I huddle into myself. One girl is brave enough to turn around and ask: "Are you the princess?"

I'm so grateful I have a cover. "No, I'm from America. I get that a lot, though." My accent convinces her it seems, even more so when Hallie appears beside me. She's even prettier in person, her hair covered by her beanie.

"Hey, Chava!" She leans in for a hug, which I return, a little surprised. Some people are so friendly. This finally seems to dissipate the whispers, though I still want to get inside in case anyone with a camera decides to snap a picture.

"Come on, I know the bouncer," Hallie tells me, grabbing my hand and pulling me from the line. We make our way to the front where she greets the bouncer, a big, burly guy named Joe who could have come straight out of a movie. He lets us through, giving Hallie a high-five. And then we're inside and the music is loud, the bass thumping. The lights are bright and neon, flashing in a way that threatens to blind me. Hallie leads me over to the bar, where things are slightly quieter, but no less crowded. She shoves her way to the front and orders a drink.

"You want anything?" she asks. I shake my head no, and she shrugs. The bartender hands her a drink, and then she turns to me, taking a sip.

"So, I have to tell you something," she says.

For a moment, I'm afraid that she knows my cover. Desperately, I search for a lie I can tell her—after all, Chava is a real person.

"I'm a DJ," she yells over the music.

My heart calms. "Oh, that's cool."

She smiles. "I brought you here 'cause I'm supposed to DJ from ten to midnight. I kind of wanted to show off, not gonna lie. Do you mind?"

Do I mind that she's about to leave me in this crowd of people all by myself? Of course I do. But I can't say that and risk pissing her off, so instead I smile.

"Of course not," I tell her. "I can't wait to hear you."

Hallie grins. "Awesome! If you want a drink, tell the bartender to put it on my tab, 'kay?" She throws back the rest of her drink, sets the glass on the bar, and notes my presence to the bartender who nods. She turns back to me, practically vibrating with excitement. "I'll come find you on my break!" She disappears before I can say anything, agreeing or otherwise. I stand beside the bar awkwardly for a moment and then begin to push my way to the other side of the crowd, where I'd seen some tall tables and chairs. Maybe I can find an empty one and just sit there for the next two hours. Great first date.

As I'm grumbling to myself and shoving through the crowd—behavior my mother would abhor—I feel a hand on my shoulder. It forcefully turns me around, and I raise my hands instinctively, though I have no idea what to do afterward. I'll just protect my face.

But I relax when I see the person: Emilia. She's wearing a sparkly bandeau top and white jeans. She smiles at me.

"What are you doing here?" she asks.

"Uh…" I can't tell her I'm on a date. She and Chava just broke up. How long is the refractory period for breakups? "I met the DJ a few days ago, and she invited me."

I point up toward the front where Hallie has taken the stage. She's taken off the rainbow beanie cap, letting her red hair flow down her back. The lights glow off her porcelain skin, her eyes closed as she gets into the song she's playing. I don't recognize it.

"Oh, that's cool," Emilia says.

"What are you doing here?" I ask.

She shrugs. "Leo and Thomas wanted to check out the club since it's new. Hey, you should come sit with us!"

"Oh, uh…" I don't know what to say. Before I can think of an excuse, she grabs me by the hand and pulls me over to her group. I stand there awkwardly as the two guys greet me, obviously familiar with Chava, but I have no idea who is who. Both are white, though one has blond hair while the other has brown. As Emilia pushes me into a seat, I try to determine who looks more like a Leo and who looks more like a Thomas.

"No drink, Chava?" the blond one asks.

"Uh, not tonight," I say. I have no idea what Chava usually drinks, but I've only ever had wine and champagne, and tonight is not the night I'm going to change that, especially not when I've got an audience.

"Oh, Thomas, I love this song," the brunette—he must be Leo, then—says. "Let's dance!"

"Sure," Thomas says, getting up from his seat. He glances at Emilia and me. "You guys gonna join?"

Emilia looks at me. I shake my head.

"Not right now," she says.

Leo shrugs. "Suit yourself."

The two guys disappear into the crowd, and then it's just Emilia and me, and I can breathe a little easier. Then, the moment of quiet drags on so long that it becomes awkward. The music is loud around us, suffocating me. We're far enough off the dance floor to avoid sweaty bodies, but a person still runs into me every now and then, their drink dangerously close to splashing on me.

"How was work today?" I ask finally.

"Oh, it was work," Emilia says, looking down at her hands.

I nod as if I know what that means.

"Did Aaron win the science fair?" she asks.

"Second place," I tell her. He wasn't happy about losing to the kid in first, but he was glad he beat everyone else, so I count that as a win. I tell Emilia as much. She laughs.

"Aaron's so smart. I'm surprised he didn't beat everyone."

"Yeah."

"Think he'll go to Purdue?"

"Oh. I, uh, I don't know." I really don't know. Is Purdue a thing for Chava's family, or is it just Chava's dream to follow in her father's footsteps?

"Sorry, I know it's a sore subject," Emilia says.

I wave a hand. "It's fine."

"So you're going to Lillard College then, right?" Emilia asks.

I shrug because I have no idea what Chava's plans are. Instead, I change the focus to Emilia. "What about you? Which university are you going to again?"

At this, Emilia dims. "Oh, um… well, I was actually meaning to talk to you about that."

My brow furrows. "What do you mean?"

"The cafe's in a lot of trouble right now," Emilia says, so quietly I can barely hear her over the music. "I don't know if my parents can afford to lose me."

"So, you're not… going?" I ask.

Emilia bites her lip. "They said I could own the cafe one day, if I wanted. I wouldn't even really need university, then."

"Is that what you want?" I ask.

"It's not always about what we want, Chava," she says, voice nearing a snap. She wrings her hands together. "Sorry, sorry. You know that. Of course you know that."

"It's okay," I say.

"I just… always had this plan, you know? School, university, job, marriage. Maybe kids, if I find the right person. But without university… is it all over with? Can anything be the same?" she asks.

"I don't know," I tell her honestly. I really don't know. For me, my life has always been planned—marriage at eighteen, the crown at thirty. There would be some endeavors in between, but nothing I really got to decide. There would be handpicked topics for me to choose from, nothing unbecoming of a princess.

"Everything feels like it's falling apart," Emilia says, sighing. "I didn't feel like I could tell you."

"You can always tell me," I say, grabbing her hand.

Emilia gives a watery smile. I hadn't realized how close to tears she had been, but now, I see her eyes are turning red, tears gathering at the bottom.

"Do you want to go home?" I ask. "I can walk you."

"What about your DJ friend?" Emilia asks. The way she says it makes it sound like she knows it's a date. Still, friends come first.

"She'll understand." I take out my phone and send Hallie a message, apologizing but saying there's an emergency, and I have to leave. "Come on." I grab Emilia and wrap my arm around her shoulders. She leans her head against me as we make our way out of the club. It feels better than kissing some random girl I just met.

# CHAPTER TWENTY
## CHAVA

I SIT AT BREAKFAST, SILENTLY buttering my toast. Florence sits to my left, reading something on her phone. Brennan walks in, hair wet and sticking to his neck, with a large smile and a happy greeting.

"Good morning, Your Grace," Florence says, looking up from her phone to give him a practiced, professional smile.

I just smile awkwardly and shove my toast in my mouth. I feel crumbs stick to the corners, mixed in with the lip gloss I'd put on. I set my toast down and wipe at the crumbs with my finger. Florence shoots me a look before returning to her phone.

"Are you busy today?" Brennan asks. I look over at him, eyebrows raised.

"Me?" I ask dumbly. Who else would he be talking to? Brennan laughs. "Yes, you."

I turn to Florence. "Am I busy today?"

She puts her phone down and eyes the both of us warily.

"That depends… what are you wanting to do?" she asks.

"What are you wanting to do?" I ask Brennan.

"I was wondering if you'd like to go on a hike with me?" he says.

"Oh, um, hiking…." I look at Florence, eyes wide in a *help me* sort of way. Hiking isn't as bad as running, but I tend to avoid the outdoors.

"That sounds wonderful," Florence says, obviously ignoring my silent pleas for help. "Aisling loves the outdoors."

Well, I can't really refute that. Aisling and Brennan are going to be married; who am I to deny them future hikes together?

"I sure do," I say, turning back to Brennan.

"Great." Brennan smiles, blindingly bright. "Would you like to go after breakfast? That way Florence can have you for the rest of the day?"

"Take all the time you need, you two," Florence says. She takes a large gulp of her coffee and stands up, phone in hand. With one last smile, a particularly pointed one in my direction, she leaves.

I take another bite of my toast instead of having to talk to Brennan. He says nothing, so by the time I swallow, I know I have to speak.

"Sure," I say. "I'll just have to get changed."

"I'll meet you outside in the gardens, then. At the gazebo?" Brennan says. He is already standing up, sliding his chair into the table.

"Works for me," I say, smiling tightly. Brennan grabs an apple from the table and tosses it in the air, catching it before taking a quick bite. He gives another charming smile before jogging lightly out of the room.

I groan and drop my face onto the table. What has Florence gotten me into?

Brennan leans against the gazebo column, silhouetted against the morning sun. He's wearing basketball shorts and a gray t-shirt. His hair is pushed back from his face and tied in a short ponytail that brings a smile to my face.

"I like the style," I call out as I get closer. "You should wear your hair like that more often."

Brennan turns, though his face is shadowed from the sun.

"It's to keep it out of my face," he says. "Long hair can be annoying."

I scoff. "You're telling me." I motion to the heavy ponytail I've pulled my hair and extensions into. It weighs on my head like a pillow. I can't wait to chop it all off the second Aisling and I switch back.

Clouds pass over the sun, darkening the sky, so I can see Brennan's face better. He looks at me with amusement and something soft in his eyes.

Brennan cocks his head. "You don't like your hair long."

"It gets… cumbersome." I choose my words carefully. When Aisling returns, her hair will still be short like mine, but will she put in extensions until it's long again? Or will she keep it short and play like she needed a change? Florence made me do a hair run for Aisling with the long hair, so will she just put them in for a day?

I shake my head—not my problem. My problem is I have to go for a hike with Brennan.

"So, where are we going to hike?" I ask. He'd asked me to meet him out back, but the gardens aren't much of a hike, more of a walk. But we can't exactly call a car to come pick us up to take us somewhere back here, so what's his plan?

"I thought the woods would be nice," Brennan says.

My eyes widen. I look up, eyes zeroing in on the expanse of trees at the edge of the perfectly manicured lawns.

"Are we allowed in there?" I ask.

"Better to ask forgiveness than permission." Brennan grins and shrugs. "They're part of the palace grounds. I asked about them when I first got here. Apparently, there's a big gate separating the palace woods from the public woods. Have you never gone in them before?"

"Uh, never really had the time," I say.

"Well, first time for everything," Brennan says. He turns and starts heading toward the woods. After a moment's hesitation, I hurry after and fall into step with him. We walk to the woods in silence. It seems comfortable, but I can't help but feel a little tense.

"What if there are, like, bears?" I ask as we get closer.

Brennan laughs. "I'm sure there aren't bears in the woods, at least these parts. I think it would be a pretty big deal if a bear broke into the palace kitchens."

"I guess," I say, feeling a little ridiculous. There's nothing wrong with the woods—my dad was a big camper, so he'd go all the time with his friends and Aaron. He took me once, but I wasn't a fan of the bugs, especially the mosquitoes. I was eaten alive and itching for days.

We make it to the edge of the forest. I can see the beginning of a dirt path and feel a sense of relief washing over me. At least we won't get lost.

"Ready?" Brennan flashes a grin, and my heart squeezes uncomfortably. I clear my throat and attempt to smile back.

"Yep," I say. We start walking, loose clumps of dirt crumbling under our feet. It's a little slippery, but nothing too bad. I might have gone a little overkill with the hiking boots, especially compared to Brennan's tennis shoes. I sneak a glance down at them—a dingy white with blue accents.

The smell of the forest hits me hard as we walk further into the trees. It's like the air freshener my dad always had hanging in his car, like cedar and bergamot, but stronger and clearer. The air is crisp and cool, almost a little too cool. I shiver in my short-sleeved shirt, goosebumps raising on my bare arms.

The sun filters through the leaves, making little kaleidoscope patterns on the ground. It's quiet except for the sounds of our steps and the occasional chirps of bird calls. I don't know how long we walk for—half an hour? an hour?—but my thighs begin to burn.

We pause for a moment to drink out of the water bottle Brennan brought. I feel my cheeks heat as I watch him tip the bottle back, watching his throat work as he swallows. When he hands the bottle to me, my cheeks burn. There's something intimate about placing my mouth in the same spot his was.

There's a rustle to my right, breaking me out of my thoughts. My gaze darts to the brush beside me. It doesn't move.

"It was probably just a squirrel," Brennan says. He sounds like he's trying not to laugh. I glare at him, and it bursts out of him. I huff and roll my eyes, shoving the bottle back at him and stomping ahead. He easily catches up and brushes the back of his hand against mine. I jump a little. He pulls his hand back.

"Sorry," he says, "I didn't mean to bump you."

"It's fine."

*You can hold my hand if you want to*, I think, but then I banish the thought. What am I doing, walking alone out here with another girl's fiancé? Because as much as I might be pretending to be her, I'm not Aisling, and I never will be.

I sigh. Overhead, the sky darkens again. I look up to see gray clouds covering the sun and most of the sky.

"Is it supposed to rain today?" I ask.

"I didn't check," Brennan says. "It's been nice all week."

A harsh gust of wind blows through, thrashing my hair around my neck and face. I wrap my arms around myself to try and soak up some warmth. Brennan takes a step closer to me, and I can feel the heat radiating from his body. How is he so much warmer than me?

*Because he's just that hot*, a delirious part of my mind giggles. I internally scoff at myself. What am I, twelve?

"Should we head back?" I ask.

"Probably," Brennan says, nodding. "We don't want to get caught in a storm."

Almost as if it were waiting on his words, there's a crack of thunder and the skies open up, rain pouring down. In seconds, we're completely drenched, my hair like a wet mop on top of my head.

"Shit!" Brennan curses. "Come on!" He grabs my hand and tugs me after him, walking faster than we were hiking but slower than a jog. He easily jumps over roots and spare tree branches while I stumble behind, barely able to see in front of me.

There's a flash of lightning and another rumble of thunder. My skin is freezing and clammy; I shiver violently. Brennan looks back and pauses, stopping so quickly that I run into his back. I fight the urge to cling to him and soak up his warmth, even if he is just as wet as I am.

"I think there's a cave right there." He has to shout to be heard over the sound of the rain, pointing at a clump of trees and rocks. "We can wait out the storm in there, if that's all right?"

"I'd be fine sharing a cave with a bear," I yell back. We hurry over to the little shelter. It's a small cave that's mercifully dry, bordered on either side by large tree trunks. I pause a little at how tight it looks, but then there's another bolt of lightning and I squeeze inside. Brennan slides in next to me and sits down. The cave is so small that his knees are literally to his ears and his arms are folded into his chest. He looks like a clown in one of those tiny Volkswagens.

I wrap my arms around my legs and hug them to my chest, hunkering down to make myself as small as possible. Even so, our sides are still pressed together, the wet material of our shirts sliding against each other.

"You can—" A shiver rocks through me. "You can put your arm around me, so you're a little more comfortable."

To my surprise, Brennan blushes. "Are you sure? Because, I mean, I'm fine."

"I'm freezing over here. It's just as beneficial to me," I say.

Still, he hesitates. I huff and drag his arm from his chest and drape it over my shoulder. His skin is a little cool to the touch, but then his grip around me tightens and the warmth of his palm seeps into my shoulder. I give another involuntary shudder and burrow into his side.

"H-how are you not cold?" I ask, my teeth chattering.

Brennan shrugs. "Guess I'm just hot."

"F-funny."

He doesn't say anything else, just stares out into the rain. Lightning lights up the sky, filtering through the leaves every now and then. Slowly, warmth starts to make its way back through me, aided by Brennan's own body heat. My shivering subsides, and I relax into his side, my head lolling onto his shoulder. He stiffens a little but loosens up, keeping his arm around my shoulder.

"How long do you think it'll storm for?" I ask.

"I don't know. Maybe an hour? Hopefully not longer than that," Brennan says.

"God, what are we going to do for an hour?" I complain.

Brennan coughs awkwardly. The implication hits me immediately after, and my cheeks flame.

"Um, that's not—I didn't mean—it wouldn't even—" I splutter.

Brennan laughs. "I know what you meant."

I bite my lip so I can't put my foot in my mouth again.

"Tell me about yourself," Brennan says suddenly, turning to look at me. I'm stunned by the blue of his eyes, so clear and bright in the darkness of the cave and the storm. I can't help but let out a confused laugh.

"What do you mean?" I ask.

"I've told you about myself, my family. And I know the things there are to know about you, what everyone in the country knows about you, I guess. Your birthday, your full name, your parents, but I don't know the important stuff," he says, his words gaining speed and strength as he says them.

"Important stuff?" I repeat. "Like what?"

"Like, what's your favorite color?" he asks.

That startles another laugh out of me. "My favorite color?"

"Yes, what is it?"

I can't help but get lost in his eyes. I get so lost that the words tumble out of my mouth: "Orange."

Brennan grins. "Orange?"

That's my favorite color. I don't know Aisling's favorite color, or maybe I do but I can't think of it. All I can think of is that I want Brennan to know *me*—Chava. I suppose I should backtrack, come up with some excuse about why I can't choose a favorite color, but I don't want to.

"Orange," I say with confidence.

"Why orange?" Brennan asks.

"When I was little, I had to get my appendix taken out. My dad got me an orange dragon to have in the hospital with me," I say.

"When were you in the hospital?" Brennan asks.

I should be panicked. I should lie. But that's something that Aisling can fix. Right now, I deflect. "I like blue, too."

Brennan's brow furrows, but he lets the question go and asks a new one. "What kind of blue? There are so many shades."

"Bright blue," I say, thinking of my comforter back home. It's worn and warm and soft against my skin when I fall asleep at night. Maybe that's why I'm so drawn to Brennan's eyes—they make me think of that blue. Of that comfort. "Like your eyes."

Brennan's gaze is a focused, heady thing. My stomach twists itself into knots at his gaze.

"What's yours?" I ask, my voice no louder than a whisper. He leans down and kisses me instead of answering.

At first, his mouth is soft and hesitant against my own. But when I kiss him back, pressing against him, he surges forward, a hand coming up to cradle my face. He tastes faintly sweet, like the apple I saw him take a bite out of, and a little like rainwater. He kisses me gently, his lips moving slowly over my own.

I've kissed my fair share of people over the past few years, whether it was because I was dating them or I was drunk or it was a dare—it didn't matter. Kissing wasn't anything special to me. Physical affection wasn't anything special to me.

Kissing Emilia, when we were dating, was fun and playful and wonderful. It was different from the other kisses because I saw a future with her.

Kissing Brennan, being wrapped up in Brennan, is safe and warm and loving. But it can't be—because he isn't *my* fiancé.

Slowly, I pull back, pressing a hand against his chest to keep him in place. I let my eyes flutter open, hesitant to break the spell. Brennan's eyes are open too, and he leans his forehead against my own, our breaths mingling.

Outside, the rain slows down, then comes to a stop.

# CHAPTER TWENTY-ONE
# AISLING

THE NEXT DAY, MELISSA GOES TO work with Gracelynn, Aaron has tutoring, and Gian plays chess in the park. This leaves me all alone. Before I can talk myself out of it, I grab a purse and Chava's phone and make my way to the coffee shop where Emilia works.

She smiles at me when I walk in, the little bell above the door ringing, and I walk up to the counter to order a drink.

"The usual?" she asks.

I nod, and she begins to ring it up.

"How did you know I was working today?" Emilia asks as she moves away from the register to begin making the drink.

Oh. I hadn't even considered that Emilia might not be working, especially after what she said last night. But I can't just repeat her worries out loud in the middle of the cafe, so I lie.

"Uh, I just wanted coffee." I smile and take the drink from her when she hands it to me.

"You didn't want to see me?" Emilia's voice is sweet and teasing, but I still find myself flustered.

"I always want to see you," I blurt out. I nearly slap my hand over my mouth as soon as the words are out. Emilia looks at me, lips slightly parted.

I cough. "I'm, uh, gonna go sit down. I can wait until you're done with your shift, if you want?"

Emilia's eyes light up. "Yeah, definitely. Ooh, we should go to the festival!"

"Festival?" I ask.

"Yeah, they've been having it all week on Main Street for the princess' wedding. We should go!"

My heart skips. "For the princess?"

"Yeah, apparently, when the king and queen got married, they did the same thing. It's actually where my mom and dad met. Isn't it so romantic?"

"Yeah, that's sweet," I say. My throat feels like it's a boa constrictor, tightening more and more with each word. "Are you sure it's a good idea? I mean, with how much I look like her and—"

Emilia waves a hand. "It'll be fine. Come on! That fancy cupcake shop is supposed to have a booth, and I wanna see what crazy merch they've put the princess' face on."

"My face?" The words squeak out before I can stop them.

"Well, technically, I guess, but it's really the princess, you know that." Emilia reaches out to grab my wrist and twists her mouth into a pretty pout. "Please, Chava? What if they have bobbleheads?"

I'm too surprised to even attempt to respond, but I manage a nod. Emilia squeals in delight.

It's not even an hour later that Emilia has me by the wrist as she drags me onto Main Street. Her hand is warm and smooth, and my skin tingles everywhere she touches. Even if I think this is a very bad idea—and that Florence would kill me if she found out—I can't bring myself to regret letting her bring me here, not if it means that she'll hold my wrist like this.

Emilia heads straight for the cupcake booth she'd told me about—*Les Petits Gâteaux*. There are twelve different cupcakes out on display, spaced evenly apart on little white doilies. There are a couple of chocolate ones, and one with a lemon wedge on top. Emilia orders three, and the lady boxes her order up and hands it over. Emilia smiles and thanks her, and then we're gone.

"Which one do you want to try first?" Emilia asks, opening the box and holding it out to me.

"You can choose," I tell her, not even knowing where to start with the box of sugar.

Emilia chooses a chocolate one and takes a bite. "Mmm. That was a good choice. Here." She holds it to my mouth. My eyes widen, but I take a bite of the cupcake, very subconscious about the fact that my mouth was exactly where hers had been.

The cupcake has a cookie and cream mixture in the middle, smooth and creamy. It's delicious. We finish off the cupcake, and then Emilia carefully sets the box into her canvas bag and hooks it over her arm.

"Let's go look at the other booths." She grabs my hand and pulls me after her.

As we walk through the streets, Emilia doesn't let go of my hand once. Some kids run past with flower crowns and bubble wands, giggling and chasing each other. We pass booths that are filled of stuff with my face on it. Emilia stops at one that's selling fine china and nearly buys a plate that centers my face, roses circling it, laughing at my horrified expression. The price tag manages to talk her out of it, but I am tempted to buy it for her, just to see her smile.

The day bleeds by, the sky turning from a light blue to orange and pink to finally black, dotted with little stars. When the sun goes down, the nightlife comes out. We pass a stage where an improv group is performing, the audience laughing wildly. Musicians come out, using violins and guitars to play old folk songs I haven't heard since I was a child.

At the end of the street, there's a group of people dancing, and Emilia pulls me in. We hold hands and spin in circles, and I can't help but wish this could be my life every day.

But the more we dance and laugh, the more attention we bring to ourselves.

"Is that the princess?" someone asks. I drop Emilia's hands almost immediately. She gives me a funny look, but I avoid her gaze.

"She's from America, actually," Emilia tells the man. "But they do look a lot alike." The man drops it, perhaps too drunk to care. Emilia steps closer to me, concern in her eyes. "What was that about?"

"I stumbled," I lie. She seems to know it, but she lets it drop anyway. "I should probably get back home. It's late."

"We've stayed out later," Emilia says, laughing a little, but I don't laugh along. I can't. I don't know the times that she and Chava have stayed out late, don't have the memories to reminisce about.

"I'm trying to get along with my mom," I tell Emilia.

She frowns. "Okay, I guess."

When we leave, she doesn't reach for my hand.

# CHAPTER TWENTY-TWO
# CHAVA

WHEN I GET BACK TO AISLING'S room, I immediately hop in the shower, stripping off my wet clothes and turning the water up to a burning temperature. I step inside and stand under the stream, letting my skin become red and hot underneath it.

When it finally stings too much to bear, I turn the water down to a manageable level and lather up a loofah with the bar soap. It's taken me a few days to get used to the smell of roses, but I've found that I prefer the floral scent to my usual citrus. I might even change when I get back home, though I'll definitely stick to body wash.

I scrub viciously at my arms and legs, turning the red skin redder with the roughness of the loofah. I pause as I go to wash my face, reluctant to wipe away the taste of Brennan. I shake my head and wipe at my lips with a vengeance, bubbles of rose-scented soap slipping into my mouth. I spit it out and wash the rest of my face before rinsing off. I put the loofah back and shut the water off.

The bathroom is eerily quiet without the sound of the water pattering down, and I feel the strange urge to scream, just to hear something. I shake my head again and grab a towel, wrapping myself up in it.

I make my way back out to Aisling's room, my hair dripping down my back. I go into the closet and dig through her dresser, withdrawing a pair of shorts and a workout shirt made of some sort of stretchy material. I slip into them and begin wringing out my hair, walking back into the room.

Just as I'm about to collapse into bed, there's a knock on the door. My heart skips a beat before the door opens, and Florence appears. I deflate, then want to slap myself.

I've got to stop. This can't go on.

Florence raises her eyebrows at my appearance. "I take it you got caught in the rain?" she asks.

"Please tell me I don't have to go do something," I whine.

"Not until after lunch."

We both glance at the clock—it's only eleven. I could lay in bed for at least an hour.

"I'll take it," I say, dropping the towel on the floor and flopping face first onto the bed.

Florence comes closer and sits down on the mattress by my feet, the bed dipping under her weight.

"Did something happen on your walk?" Florence asks.

"Hike," I correct. "He said hike."

"Answer the question," she says.

"Brennan kissed me."

"I see."

I remain silent for a moment, weighing what I'm about to say in my mind. "I kissed him back."

"And how was it?"

I flip over and sit up, staring at Florence. She stares right back at me, unperturbed.

"That's all you have to say?" I demand.

"Well, I think that your feelings on the matter are important."

"But they shouldn't be!"

Florence tilts her head. "Why not?"

"Because—because I'm not her! I'm not—this isn't my life! I'm making choices for her that she wouldn't make. I'm ruining her life, aren't I?"

"Just because you kissed the duke doesn't mean her life is ruined."

"But I don't want to lead him on, promise him things she can't give. I'm being selfish." I cross my arms over my chest, holding myself together. I really have been selfish—with Emilia, with Aisling, with Brennan. It's like I can't stop myself from taking everything from everyone. Tears sting my eyes at thought, and I angrily wipe them away.

Florence watches me silently, eyes calculating.

"You don't have to be so worried," she says. "Aisling can handle things when she gets back."

"She left to try and be free, even if just for a few days," I say, "but how will she feel when she comes back and her cage is tighter than ever before? Because of me?"

Florence sighs. "You're being over dramatic. It's not like the duke is in love with you. People don't fall in love that quickly."

I say nothing to that. Brennan couldn't possibly be in love with me—Aisling—I know that. But he feels something, and it makes my stomach churn with guilt.

"You said that you were married," I say to Florence, remembering the comment she'd said in passing, as if it were no big deal. Off to the side, she stiffens.

"How did you know you were in love with them?" I ask.

Florence gives a bitter smile. "I didn't. Or, I thought I did. But after a year of marriage, I realized that I didn't. It was a foolish decision, one I'd made without really thinking about the consequences."

"Who were they?" I ask.

"Just a boy I knew when I was young," she said. "Our families pushed us together, and we thought they knew best."

"What changed?"

"I did. I met… a girl." Florence lets out a harsh laugh and puts her hands to her face. "Oh, God. I've never told anyone that before."

That surprises me.

"Wait, what? Never? Not even Aisling?" I ask.

"I wasn't ready," Florence admits.

"Why are you telling me, then?"

"Aisling can trust you with her secret." Florence smiles sadly. "I figured I can trust you with mine."

"Where's the girl? Is she at the palace?" I ask.

Florence's smile falters. "No, she's gone. She left. While I was still married, I was accepted to be Aisling's lady-in-waiting. The divorce was already a strike against me, and being in such a public position… not to mention my family… I guess I just wasn't brave enough." Florence stares at her hands in her lap, folded primly together.

"That's why I was so willing to let Aisling have this week," Florence continues. "I wanted her to get to be herself, in some capacity. I know she's pretending to be you, but getting to be out and proud—I wanted that for her. I *want* that for her. I wish she could be herself here."

"Why can't she?" I ask.

"It's different for her," Florence says. "She has expectations piled onto her, not just from her family but from an entire country. She can't afford to fumble, and in a country that's primarily Catholic… I just want her to be okay."

"But is she okay?" I ask. "Having to hide who she truly is? Having to marry someone she knows she can never love?"

"I hope one day she'll tell the duke the truth, but that's her decision," Florence says.

"That wasn't what I asked," I say, but Florence stands up and heads for the door, her posture perfectly straight. She pauses at the frame, though, back turned to me.

"I can't push her because I can't know I'll be there to catch her," Florence says. "That's something you'll never understand." She leaves, letting the door shut softly behind her.

# CHAPTER TWENTY-THREE
## AISLING

I WAKE UP AFTER THE SUN has risen, a first for me in as long as I can remember. I feel around the nightstand for Chava's phone. My fingers find purchase with the cold screen, and I grab it. Clicking the phone on, I see it's a little after eight in the morning. I let the phone drop to my chest and close my eyes. I almost want to fall back asleep, which is unlike me. My energy has been dragging the past few days. Is it because I know I have to go back to the palace tonight, go back to pretending to be perfect all of the time?

I sigh and pull myself out of bed, setting the phone back on the nightstand. I pull on a pair of Chava's denim shorts and a spaghetti-strap tank top—it's an outfit I'd never get to wear as Aisling, and I relish the rasp of the denim against my thighs. I run a brush through my short hair and slip on a pair of Converse before heading out of Chava's room and down the stairs.

The smell of French toast fills the air as I get closer to the kitchen, thick and syrupy.

"Chava, is that you?" Melissa calls out, voice filtering through the doorway.

"Yeah," I say, reaching the door. "Good morn—" I cut myself off. Emilia sits at the table, a plate in front of her. She smiles at me.

"Hey, your mom was just about to wake you up for me," she says.

I turn to Melissa. "Oh?"

"Emilia said she wanted to talk to you before she had work," Chava's mom says.

"What time do you work?" I ask Emilia.

"Nine-thirty. So we've got some time. Come have breakfast with me." Emilia's smile is so, so easy and so, so pretty. Before my brain catches up with my body, I sit down beside her. Melissa comes over with a stack of French toast and a knowing smile.

"I'll see if I can go wake up Aaron," Melissa announces. "You two dig in." She disappears before I can say anything else. I glance nervously at Emilia, who laughs a little and gives a one-armed shrug. I grab my fork and pick up three thick pieces of French toast. I cut off a corner of one piece and shove it in my mouth so I can't talk before reaching for the butter for the rest of the slices.

"Are you okay?" Emilia asks, picking up her own piece of French toast.

"'M fine," I mumble through a mouthful of eggy bread.

She doesn't say anything else, but she does have a small smile on her face as she goes about eating her own breakfast. Melissa comes down, followed by Aaron a few minutes later, his hair still mussed from sleep. They join us at the table, and the kitchen is filled with clinks of silverware against plates and the soft sound of chewing.

Much too soon, my plate is empty, and so is Emilia's. I'm tempted to take another piece of French toast—maybe three—but I think that might make me throw up, so I don't risk it. I grab Emilia's plate and my own and take them over to the sink to rinse off.

"Oh, I'll get those, Chava," Melissa says. "I don't want to keep Emilia from work."

"I've got time," Emilia assures her.

Melissa smiles. "It's fine. I'll clean up."

Emilia turns back to me. "Do you want to take a walk?"

I swallow hard. "Sure."

We say goodbye to Chava's mom and Aaron and head out the front door. For the first few minutes, we walk in silence, our hands brushing every now and then. My heart beats quickly, the thumping loud in my ears. I miss a step when Emilia suddenly grabs my hand and laces our fingers together.

I look at our hands, wide-eyed. "What are you—"

"I've been thinking a lot about this," Emilia says, slowing to a stop. "You've been different this past week, a good different. Not that how you were before wasn't good, that's not what I'm saying. Just—ugh. This went so much smoother in my head." Emilia lets her head fall back and groans.

My stomach is twisted in knots—this can't be happening. This is my best dream and my worst nightmare. Emilia is someone I never expected to meet but am so glad I did—but she hasn't met me, not as Aisling. Whatever she's about to say, it's going to affect Chava's life, not mine.

Emilia straightens up and smiles nervously at me.

"I would like to give us a try again," she says.

I suck in a quick breath. Her brown eyes bore into mine, so tender and warm and inviting. I want to fall into them, want to curl up in the comfort that they offer. I blink the thoughts away.

Emilia is still staring at me, her smile slowly falling.

"Don't!" I say, holding my hands up. She jumps, and I wince. Too much. "I mean, it's just—You don't understand—"

"No, I do understand." Where before, Emilia's face was open and honest, now it's brittle and practiced.

"No, you really don't. I want to, I truly do, but I—I can't." I cut myself off before I can say anything more. I'm on my last day as Chava, I can't possibly fail now, at the finish line.

"Why not?" Emilia frowns. "I'm not trying to be pushy or anything. You said no, and I respect that, but I don't understand what you're saying."

"I'm not… this isn't me," I say, biting my lip.

Emilia quirks an unimpressed eyebrow.

"This week has been different because I've been looking at it differently, but I can't promise that I'll be the same next week."

Her brows furrow. "That doesn't make any sense."

"People change?" I try.

"And you have," Emilia says. "Are you saying that you're going to change… back?"

My eyes widen to what I'm sure is a comical size. "N-no! Yes? It's complicated. Don't you have work soon?"

Emilia looks at me suspiciously. "You have been acting differently, almost like a different person. You barely showed any emotion on Wednesday, and I just figured it was a grief thing… But maybe it was because you never knew Chava's dad," she says.

I let out a laugh, which probably isn't as convincing as I want it to be.

Emilia's eyes widen. "Oh my God, you're the princess."

I flinch, looking around. We're still in a residential area—only a few blocks down from

Chava's house—in the middle of a sidewalk. Anyone could walk by and hear everything. Emilia doesn't seem to care.

"Holy *shit!*" she says. "You're actually the princess. All those times I defended you and said you *weren't* the princess when actually… actually you *were!*"

"Shh!" I try to shush her, but Emilia is having none of it.

"Wait, wait, wait, if you're pretending to be Chava, is Chava pretending to be *you?*"

"Yes." This time, my answer is more confident. When the conversation is focused on Chava, it's much easier to have.

"So, Chava's at the palace? Doing princess things? My Chava?"

The distinction—*My Chava*—stings.

"Yes, we switched places for the week," I say.

"But… *why?*" Emilia looks so shell-shocked. I can practically see the thoughts racing in her head, trying to come up with an answer.

"Chava needed help getting into Purdue," I lie, deliberately leaving myself out of the equation. And it's partially true. She just got that bonus *after* I accosted her in the back alley of a dress shop.

"But what about you? Why did *you* switch? I mean, you're the princess. What could you possibly get out of this?" Emilia asks.

"Being a princess isn't all it's cracked up to be," I say.

Emilia scoffs. "Don't come at me with that *oh, woe is me, my perfect life is so hard* bullshit. You've got things most people in this country can only dream of having. So, cut the crap, and spill."

I bite my lip. My stomach flips at the thought of telling her the truth, but… I like Emilia. I *really* like her, more than just thinking she's pretty or graceful. I think she's funny and smart and that she has a cute snorty laugh. I think she might be the only girl I ever have a chance of getting to know, of getting to maybe fall in love with.

"I, um, I," I stutter. I pause, close my eyes, and take a deep breath. "I like girls. I'm a lesbian."

Emilia blinks. "Oh. So, why are you marrying the duke?"

She says it like it's no big deal, like it's something I have a choice in. I let out a bitter laugh.

"It's not that simple," I tell her.

"Okay, it's not that simple, then," Emilia says. "But I still don't get it. What do you get out of this week?"

"I wanted to kiss a girl," I say quietly. "I wanted to talk to girls. I wanted to try to be myself."

"You can't be that all the time?" Emilia asks.

"No, no, I can't," I say.

Emilia frowns, and when she looks at me, I see pity in her eyes. It makes me want to scream.

"So, all of this, this week, was a lie?" Emilia asks.

"I don't—I don't know."

Emilia looks away, her hands turning into fists at her sides. She laughs a little .

"I can't believe this," she says. "I can't believe you tricked me like this! I told you things, and I thought I was telling Chava, but instead, I was telling *you!* You *lied* to me! You *used* me!"

"No," I say, but she cuts me off.

"So, this was all some little game to you? Pretend to be Chava and play with my heart, knowing that when she comes back, whenever she comes back… what?"

"I don't know!"

Emilia turns back, and now, there are tears where pity used to be. The tables have turned. "What do you have to say for yourself? Was any of it real?"

My throat is thick, so thick I can barely speak. "I can't," I manage to croak out. I feel tears burn at the corners of my eyes. "I—I have to go."

I turn and run. I can't bear to look back at Emilia. I'm not brave enough to see her face.

# CHAPTER TWENTY-FOUR
## CHAVA

To avoid Brennan, I have breakfast sent up to my room. I poke at the perfectly cooked eggs with the tines of my silver fork, watching the yolk break and spill across the plate. The yellow flows over the blue floral pattern, turning green. I smear the yolk on the tines and bring it up to my mouth.

There's a knock on the door—a knock I've come to realize is special to Florence only—and she enters, closing it behind her. She gives me an unimpressed look, sitting at Aisling's little antique dining table with my plate of food.

"Really?" she asks, voice dry. She's got a clipboard in her arms and her phone in her left hand. Her dark hair is pulled up in a tight bun, the baby hairs smoothed down her temples with gel, and she wears a bright red lipstick that stands out against her brown skin.

"What?" I ask, shoving a bite of egg into my mouth.

Florence frowns. "This is your solution? To avoid the duke?"

"It worked in seventh grade with Tommy Newman," I tell her. That had been an embarrassing two weeks. Tommy had been in three of my seven classes, so I'd bribed and cajoled my classmates into switching seats so that he and I were on opposite ends of the classroom; at lunch, I'd made my friends form a protective circle around me; and I'd never been more glad to not have recess. Finally, on the first day of the third week, Tommy had come to school with a buzzcut, and it had effectively killed any budding feelings I'd had.

I doubted I would be so lucky with Brennan. But I had one thing going for me—I'd never see the guy again after today.

"This is not some schoolgirl crush," Florence says.

"It absolutely is," I say, latching onto this excuse. "I think he's hot, that's it. There's nothing else that is attracting me to him."

Florence lets out an exasperated sigh.

"It's not healthy to suppress your feelings like this," she tells me matter-of-factly.

"I can't like him," I say. "I just broke up with my girlfriend because—because I'm not capable of love right now."

At this confession, Florence walks over to me. She sets her clipboard on the table and takes the other seat at the table, cocking her head at me.

"What does that mean?" she asks. "Did this girl tell you that?"

"No, I mean, not really. It's just—it's true."

"How is it true?"

"My heart isn't right, right now, after everything with my dad's death and my mom—that's complicated," I tell her. "My heart, it's just, like, broken. I only have pieces of it to give, not the whole thing."

"And what's wrong with giving pieces?" Florence asks.

"Isn't it selfish?" I ask.

"I think it's healing." Florence folds her hands in front of her and leans on the table. "Chava, you lost someone very close to you, someone you loved very much. But that doesn't mean you stop living or stop loving. It's okay if you can't put your whole heart in a relationship right away, as long as it's in the right place. Love isn't linear. There's no set way to do it or a timeline of how long it should take. You know your heart best, and if you're able to give pieces, give pieces. And if someone isn't happy with just pieces right away, that's okay because that's their right. But it's your right to only give pieces, too."

I blink, trying to wrap my head around everything that Florence just said to me.

"You think I should give Brennan a piece?" I ask.

Florence's face turns pained. "If you were a different person, and so was he, then I would say yes. But as it is… you obviously can't."

I bite my lip and look down at my plate. "Right."

"But that doesn't mean you can't give a piece to someone else one day," Florence says, reaching out for my hand. She grips it tightly, and I look back up at her in surprise. "It's a good sign that you feel this way for Brennan, and I wish it could be different for you two."

"It's fine, Florence," I say, hoping she'll drop the subject. She doesn't look keen to, but before she can say anything else, her phone rings. She gives me a meaningful look and holds up a finger in a *Wait one minute* sort of way.

"Hello?" Florence answers. "Yes… Isn't this a little late… No, of course I can make time… Yes, we'll see you in half an hour." She hangs the phone up and presses it against her forehead.

"What?" I ask, anxiety mixing with dread in my stomach.

"Get ready. The queen wants to see you."

Florence puts me in a light pink sleeveless dress and simple sandals. I'm thankful I don't have to try and navigate the hallways in a pair of Aisling's heels. I'm capable of walking in heels, but I'm also nervous—I could definitely see myself plummeting face first down a set of stairs.

Florence and I make our way through the family wing to the queen's private sitting room. Florence knocks politely on the door and takes a step back so she's standing behind my right shoulder. After a minute, one of the large white doors open, and a middle-aged white woman with her strawberry blonde hair up in a messy updo pokes her head out. Her eyes light up when she sees us.

"Oh, good, you're here! Thank you, Florence, for always being so on top of things. Come in, Your Highness. Your mother is getting dressed," the woman says. She opens the door more and ushers me through, Florence following behind. I glance back at her, eyes questioning. She shrugs.

The woman leads me to a vintage-looking couch with white-and-blue striped cushions. I sit down as lady-like as possible, crossing my ankles like Aisling demonstrated so long ago and Florence drilled into me twenty minutes ago. Florence stands behind the couch, posture perfectly straight, almost militaristic.

"Aisling, is that you?" The voice floats from behind a white wooden partition. It must be the queen.

I fight the urge to throw up. "Yes."

The queen appears beside the partition, dressed in a pale blue dress with long, drapey sleeves and a full skirt. She gives a little twirl as she comes toward me. As she gets closer, I realize she's going in for a hug.

Automatically, I stiffen, but I force myself to relax as I stand up and meet her embrace. She wraps me in her arms and places my head on her shoulder.

Relief floods me when she releases me from her grasp. I smooth down my skirt and sit back down on the couch. The queen continues to stand and holds her arms out to her sides.

"Well?" she asks. "What do you think?"

I look back at Florence, then quickly turn back to the queen. "Uh, about what?"

"My mother-of-the-bride dress!" she says.

My eyes widen in realization. "Oh, right! Right, it's so pretty!"

"Isn't it perfect?" It's a rhetorical question because she barely takes a breath before she speaks again. "Gracelynn is just incredible, don't you think?"

"Yes, she's great," I say.

"How is your dress? I'm sad that I haven't gotten to see it yet, but I do like the idea of seeing it for the first time on your wedding day," the queen says.

"Oh, it's great. Really beautiful," I tell her.

The queen laughs and turns to Florence. "What do you think of it, Florence?"

"It's unlike anything I've ever seen. Gracelynn has really outdone herself. Aisling looks like a bride," Florence says. I'm surprised at the emotion in her voice. It strikes me that Florence has known Aisling since she was a young girl, that this whole event is probably just as meaningful to her as it is to the queen or to Aisling herself. Even if Aisling isn't marrying for love, she's still taking a big step into adulthood. Her life will be forever changed.

The queen's voice matches Florence's. "Our girl is growing up, isn't she?" The queen sits down beside me and cups my chin in her hands. "You're going to make such a lovely bride, my darling. I absolutely can't wait."

She wipes her eyes carefully, mindful of her mascara, and shakes her head. When she looks at me, her face is fresh and happy.

"So, how has this past week been with the duke?" she asks.

I swallow hard. "Fine."

The queen gives me a look that is so like the one my mother gave me when I was dating my first girlfriend and tried to downplay it. I have to hold back a laugh at the comparison—the queen of a nation and my mother, an assistant at a dress shop, giving their daughters the same expression.

"Fine? That's all you have to say about him?" the queen asks.

"What do you want me to say?" I ask.

"I want to know how you two have been getting along, if there are any sparks." She raises her eyebrows expectantly, and my eyes widen.

"Uh, no, no sparks," I lie. "But he's nice, and kind. He'll make a great partner."

The queen's face falls. "Oh."

"Isn't that good?" I ask.

She sighs. "I'd just hoped… I know your father and I are pushing you into this, with the law and everything, but I had hoped you would find love with the duke."

I nearly choke on my spit. Love, after one week? Was this woman crazy?

It's as if the queen reads my mind.

"I know it might sound crazy, and it certainly wasn't like that for your father and I—it took us a few years before we fell in love. But I'd wanted better for you, Aisling." The queen reaches out to smooth my hair, brushing a stray strand behind my ear. She leaves her hand on my face, cupping my cheek.

"What if—what if I can't love the duke?" I ask. Out of the corner of my eye, I see Florence stiffen. I internally roll my eyes—does she really think I'm going to out Aisling to her own mother before she's ready? No way in hell is that my place.

The queen's hand falls from my face. "What do you mean?"

"I just mean, what if we never fall in love? What then?"

"You just have to put in the work, darling, that's all," the queen assures me. "Love will come with time."

"But what if it doesn't?" I ask. She keeps side-stepping my question, ignoring the meaning underneath it, too. But she knows what I'm really asking.

The queen stiffens. "Why are you asking this? I thought you said the duke was perfectly nice."

"Him being nice doesn't mean I'm going to fall into his arms and we're going to ride off into the sunset," I say. "Why are you so determined that we fall in love?"

"Because I want you to be happy!" Her voice is like a whip, snapping through the air.

"I don't need a man to be happy," I say, keeping my voice calm even though I want to shout. Is this all that the queen thinks Aisling needs, some random guy she's never even met?

The queen takes a deep breath and lets it out slowly. "I don't know where all of this is coming from, Aisling, but I do hope that you'll drop it."

I want to scream. I want to throw things. I want to shake the queen until she realizes her daughter will never be happy with this wedding they've arranged for her.

But I don't. I can't. I've probably already said too much, acted too unlike Aisling to push anymore. Instead, I take a breath.

"I just don't want you to feel guilty," I say finally, "if this doesn't end up like you imagined. Brennan and I aren't you and Dad." I choke a little on referring to the king so casually, but I make it through.

Instead of looking understanding, however, the queen lights up. "You call him Brennan? Does he call you Aisling?"

"Yes? We're going to be married tomorrow. There's no point in formalities, is there?" I ask. Have I done something wrong in referring to Brennan so casually, in letting him refer to me the same?

The queen just bites her lip and nods at me. She stands up and clasps her hands together. "Well, I just wanted to catch up with you a bit and show you my dress. I'll let you get back to whatever it is you're doing today." This last part is aimed toward Florence, who nods professionally. "And I'm so excited for the rehearsal dinner tonight. Everything is feeling so real, wouldn't you agree?"

"Yes," I say.

I stand up from the couch and let Florence lead me to the door as the queen disappears back behind the partition. The strawberry-blonde, who I assume to be the queen's aide, suddenly appears to open the door for us.

"We'll see you at seven o'clock, sharp!" the woman says cheerfully, but there's a glint in her eyes that warns me not to be late anyway. Florence nods her assent as we leave the room and start heading down the hall back to Aisling's. She says nothing, so neither do I.

Once back in Aisling's room though, the door safely shut and locked, Florence turns on me.

"What was that?" she demands.

"I just wanted the queen to understand what she was doing to her only child," I say, crossing my arms across my chest.

"The queen is a good mother," Florence tells me.

"I never said she wasn't," I say, "but she's certainly not the most attentive or observant."

"That was not your place," Florence says.

"I was standing up for Aisling and setting the stage for the rest of her life. You and I both know she'll never fall in love with Brennan. And that's not her fault, so why not set the expectation beforehand?"

Florence's nostrils flare, her eyes flashing. But, after a moment, she relents.

"That was risky," she says finally.

"Believe me, I know." I shiver. Despite Florence's assurances that there are no dungeons in this palace, I'm still not convinced. "But it's fine. It's over. Now, I just have to hide out here until Aisling gets back, which will be before the dinner, right?"

"Six o'clock," Florence says, nodding her assent.

I let out a breath. I'm so ready for this week to be over.

# CHAPTER TWENTY-FIVE
# AISLING

Melissa attacks me as soon as I walk through the front door.

"So, what did Emilia want?" she asks, unable to hold back her excitement.

The words get stuck in my throat. She continues to look at me expectantly. I swallow hard and manage to get the words out.

"She wanted to get back together," I say.

Melissa squeals. My eyes widen. She wraps me in her arms and squeezes tightly.

"What did you say?" she asks, letting go of me.

I bite my lip, trying to come up with an answer. I hadn't actually said no, rather that I couldn't, and then I'd come clean about the whole switch thing, which I couldn't very well do with Melissa…

Melissa's face falls as she waits for me to answer. "You said no?"

I look down at my shoes. "Yeah." "But why? You two have been so happy this past week. You've been hanging out, and she was so supportive at the fundraiser, and wasn't she the one who broke up with you?"

"I mean, kind of? It was sort of mutual. We broke up because of… Papa."

Melissa's brows furrow. "Papa? What does that mean?"

I shrug. "I guess I wasn't being a very good girlfriend." I'm unsure of the exact reasons that Chava and Emilia broke up, but from what Chava told me, that was the gist of it: Emilia thought Chava was too grief-stricken to be in a new relationship.

"Well, to be fair, it was your first serious relationship," Melissa says, leading me into the kitchen and setting me down at the table. "It might have been a little ambitious to take on after Papa died."

I nod, uncertain of what to say next, so I say nothing. Melissa just holds my hand on the table.

"You're okay with Emilia and me?" I ask suddenly.

Melissa blinks. "Of course, I am. Why wouldn't I be?"

"Because, well, because I'm a girl and… she's a girl," I trail off.

"Chava, haven't we already been over this?" Melissa asks.

"Maybe I need reminding." I haven't been able to look her in the eye this whole time, just staring at her hand over mine, but at my words, she pulls her hand back. I think, wildly, that I've just ruined everything.

But instead, Melissa's gentle voice tells me to look at her. I do.

"Like I told you when you were fourteen and you said you had a crush on Sally Greenfield, I will love you no matter who you love. I loved you through Sally, then Finn, even if those were only for a few weeks. I loved you through Emilia. And I will love you no matter who else holds your heart.

"Nothing would break my heart more than knowing you weren't being true to yourself, especially because of me. I want you to be whoever you want to be, and I want you to love whoever you want to love."

"I think I need to go talk to Emilia," I say, standing up. Melissa's face lights up, and I hurry to add, "I don't know if we'll get back together, but I do need to tell her something."

Perhaps, once Chava gets back, Emilia will want to get back together with Chava, even if she has spent the past week with me. The thought stings, but I know I have to give myself a chance anyway. The Chava that Emilia wants to get back together with is me, so maybe… she wants me, too?

I enter the cafe to find it much busier than I've ever seen it. I make my way to the counter, looking for Emilia. Instead, a white man in his mid-twenties stands at the counter, taking orders. He looks up and catches my eye, his face lighting up in recognition.

"She's in the back!" he yells over the music and the bustle of the room.

"Thanks!" I yell at him and begin to make my way to the back of the cafe. I haven't been this far back, sticking to the areas beside the large glass windows that let lots of sunlight in. But it's brightly lit back here, despite the dark wood that makes up the booths lining the walls and the tables filling in the middle space. There's a swinging door marked *Employees Only*, but the guy had said I could come back here, so I only hesitate a little before pushing the door open and sliding through.

The little kitchen area they have back here is like a miniature version of the one in the palace, all stainless-steel and shiny. Emilia stands with her back to me, bent over and working on something in front of her. There's another woman who looks like an older version of Emilia, with dark skin and dark hair piled up onto her head and out of her way. The woman looks up when I enter, and she smiles warmly.

"Chava, I didn't expect to see you," she says.

Emilia stiffens and turns to look at me, holding a piping bag of something in her hand. A glob of it drips from the tip and falls onto the floor with a soft *splat*.

"I'm sorry to interrupt," I say, "I just needed to talk to Emilia for a minute."

"Well, go on, then. Emilia, take her out back. You're due for a break anyway," the woman says.

"But Mum, I'm in the middle of making these macarons you wanted," Emilia protests.

"They'll be fine for a few minutes," Emilia's mother says. Emilia sighs and sets the piping bag down on the counter. She unties the apron from around her and lays it beside the piping bag. Without looking at me, she begins to make her way through the kitchen. Hurriedly, I follow after her.

Eventually, we reach a large stainless-steel door that Emilia pushes open. It leads to an alley with a few boxes lined up on either side and a dumpster a few feet down. Emilia turns immediately and crosses her arms, cocking a hip.

"What do you want, Princess?" she asks.

I wince. I can't tell if the word is meant to be an address or if she's making fun of me, but it makes me ache either way.

"Look, I'm sorry you feel that you've been tricked," I begin.

Emilia cuts me off. "I don't feel as if I've been tricked. I *was* tricked."

"Okay, you're right. We did trick you, but it wasn't done maliciously. Neither Chava nor I were thinking about who it would affect, just that we needed to get out of our lives for a few days. And these past few days, especially the ones with you, were some of the best of my life," I say honestly.

Emilia blinks, shocked. I forge forward before she can say anything else.

"I know you thought I was Chava this whole time, but I've always known it was you. And I've always been astounded by what I've seen and gotten to experience with you. You're extremely intelligent and funny and caring and beautiful. God, you're probably the most beautiful girl I've ever seen. And I know I can't do anything about this, even if you wanted to, because I'm getting married tomorrow, but I didn't want to continue on this path without first telling you how I felt. Feel. How I feel, because I really like you, Emilia. And I don't expect you to like me back, especially because I'm sure your feelings are all jumbled, but mine aren't. I needed you to know that."

I stand there for a moment after I've said my piece, waiting for her to respond. Emilia just looks shell-shocked.

My phone rings before anything else can happen. I look down to see that it's Melissa, and a heavy feeling settles in my stomach.

I answer the phone. "Hello?"

"Chava? We have to go to the hospital," she says, frantic.

"What? Why? What's going on?" I ask.

"Aaron's in the hospital," Melissa says.

My blood chills. "What happened?"

"He was over at a friend's, and he had an allergic reaction to something. We don't know what it was, but it was so bad they had to call an ambulance. They said he couldn't breathe, and he was unconscious."

"Which hospital?" I ask.

"Children's hospital. I'm almost at the cafe," she says. I can hear tears in her voice, and my own throat closes up.

"The cafe?" I ask.

"To pick you up," she says. "We'll head to the hospital after."

"Why don't I meet you there?" I ask. I need to call Chava and let her know, and then she can head to the hospital and I can head back to the palace. If Melissa picks me up, there's no way to get out of her sight.

"I'm literally a block away, Chava. Meet me out front." The phone clicks off, and the dial tone beeps in my ear.

"Shit," I curse under my breath.

"What's happening? Who's in the hospital?" Emilia asks.

"Aaron. Melissa's coming to pick me up," I say. "I have to get a hold of Chava, we have to figure something out."

"Give me the number," Emilia says. "I'll call her and let her know."

"But—"

"Give me the phone." She holds her hand out, and I give her Chava's phone on autopilot.

"You're just going to have to be his big sister right now." Emilia grabs me by the shoulders and steers me back inside. Emilia's mom calls out to us as we pass by, but Emilia shouts something about Aaron and the hospital and keeps pushing me forward.

When I make it out front, Melissa's car sits in the street, and I run for it. I slide into the passenger seat and buckle up. Melissa's face is tear streaked, and she reaches out for my hand. I grab it tightly as we head for the hospital.

# CHAPTER TWENTY-SIX
# CHAVA

Aisling calls me in the early afternoon.

"Aaron's in the hospital."

My mind spins with the new information—that's not Aisling's voice, and my brother's in the hospital.

"Who—who is this?" I ask, my voice shaky.

"Emilia," she says. "Aisling told me everything."

I choose to ignore that and focus on Aaron. "Why is Aaron in the hospital?"

"I'm not sure. Your mom called Aisling, but I couldn't hear much. Your mom picked her up, and they're on their way to the hospital now," Emilia says.

"I have to go." I look around the room wildly, searching for some way to escape. It hits me hard that there's nothing I can do, not without Florence. And even then, how would I manage to sneak out of the palace without Aisling already here? And how would Aisling leave the hospital without me already there? "I can't go."

"Everything will be fine," Emilia says.

"Everything is not fine!" I snap. "My brother is in the hospital, and Aisling has no way of getting here to switch back. We have to switch back *tonight*. She's getting married *tomorrow*!"

"Well, maybe you should never have switched places to begin with," Emilia bites back.

I pause and swallow hard.

"It's not that simple," I say. "Aisling—"

"Aisling told me her reasons," Emilia cuts me off.

I bite my lip. "I don't know why you're so mad."

Emilia lets out a bitter laugh. "Chava! You're running away from your problems instead of facing them!"

"I did this to help Aisling," I argue.

"And skipping out on the fundraiser was just a bonus?" Emilia asks.

"You don't get it," I say. "You never have. This is my grief, and I get to handle it how I want."

"Even if it hurts others?"

"My mom doesn't know, and I've already talked to Aaron. No one was ever supposed to know. This is honestly just falling apart. It wasn't supposed to be like this."

"Well, this is what it's become," Emilia says.

I shake my head, even though she can't see me. "I can't deal with this right now, Emilia. If you want to yell at me, yell at me tomorrow. Right now, I need to find out what's going on with my brother, and I need to get a hold of Aisling."

"Fine," Emilia says, though her voice has softened. "Everything will be okay, Chava. I'm sure it will."

I don't say anything when I hang up. I'm not sure I believe her.

❧

Florence walks through Aisling's door not even ten minutes after I text her the SOS.

"What's going on?" she asks, foregoing any greetings.

"My brother is in the hospital, and Aisling is there with him," I say.

Florence's eyes widen. "What's wrong with your brother?"

"I have no idea," I say. "I'm freaking out."

"Hey, hey, it's okay," Florence says soothingly. "We can call Aisling and figure this out."

"No, we can't. Emilia has her phone—*my* phone," I say.

"Wait, so who called you?" Florence asks.

"Emilia. Aisling told her about the switch, but that's not important! The important thing is that my brother is in the hospital, and I have no way of finding out which hospital or how to get to him!" I say.

Florence closes her eyes and brings her hands to her temples, rubbing them in circles.

"You girls are going to give me gray hairs," she mutters to herself.

"Florence!" I snap. "What are we going to do?"

"Okay, so let me get this straight. Aisling is at the hospital with your brother, but we don't know which hospital, let alone which floor and room. Aisling is probably there with your mother, leaving Aisling no way to get back here to switch with you. And we can't let you leave to go switch with her because Aisling isn't allowed to leave the palace, and if someone were to come looking for her and find her missing... Let's just say it wouldn't be good." The more Florence speaks, the more my heart sinks to the floor.

"So, what do we do?" I ask.

Florence eyes me with more than a little bit of sympathy. "We get you ready for the rehearsal dinner."

"No, no way in hell," I say. I back away from her, as if she's going to jump up and wrap me in rope.

"Chava, we have no choice," Florence says.

"Tell them I'm sick," I say desperately.

"The wedding is tomorrow, and Aisling's mother saw you a few hours ago."

"It's pre-wedding jitters."

"That's not going to work."

"I can't pretend to be some fancy, well-mannered princess in front of all those people. They'll see right through me!"

"You can do it," Florence says. She grabs me by the wrist and moves her hand down to hold mine. "You have to do it."

"But I don't want to," I whine.

Florence's eyes narrow. "Too bad. While you're at dinner, I'll see if I can find where Aaron is at and what's wrong. Hopefully, I can get into contact with Aisling by then, too."

"And if you can't? What do we do then?" I ask.

"I will," Florence says. The words seem confident, but I can see the uncertainty in her eyes. She ushers me to the closet and toward picking out a dress before I can ask any more questions. I've got a terrible feeling this switch is about to come crashing down around the both of us.

# CHAPTER TWENTY-SEVEN
# AISLING

When we get to the hospital, they won't let us see Aaron. Melissa talks with the doctor while I go downstairs to wait for Gian. He was getting a ride from one of his book club members, according to Melissa.

Gian hurries through the sliding doors, looking around frantically. When he sees me, he rushes over and wraps me in a hug, his arms surprisingly strong for someone so skinny.

"Where's your mother?" he asks.

"Upstairs, talking to the doctor," I tell him. "I don't know what they're doing, but they won't let us see Aaron." I can hear the hysteria in my voice, something I don't have to fake. I never thought I would grow this attached to random people in such a short amount of time, but the terror on Gian and Melissa's faces sent shivers throughout my body. I can't help but picture Aaron, frail and lifeless, hooked up to a million tubes in a hospital bed.

Gian breathes out through his nose and nods.

"Okay," he says. "Okay. We need to remain calm. Let's go to the cafeteria and get some tea. When was the last time you ate?"

"This morning," I tell him. My stomach rumbles as if to agree. Gian nods again. He has me text Melissa to join us when she's done talking with the doctor, then he leads me to the cafeteria on the first floor of the hospital.

The cafeteria is exactly like in the television shows I've seen, how I've always pictured it—the linoleum floors, the fluorescent lights, the round tables at various intervals around the space. There's a long, metal counter with food laid across it under heating lamps. People in scrubs and regular clothes alike go down the line, grabbing foil-wrapped items and ringing them up at the end with the cashier.

"Go get something to eat," Gian tells me, handing me his credit card. I take it, looking down at the piece of plastic in my hand: Gian Laghari—why does that last name sound familiar?

"What about you and Mama?" I ask.

"We'll get something when your mother gets down here," he assures me, then pushes me toward the line. I go through it on autopilot, picking up the first things I see— a grilled cheese and a basket of fries. I get water from the fridge as well and pay the cashier before joining Gian at the table he's chosen.

Melissa finds us after about ten minutes, her face worn and wearied. Gian stands up and embraces her before ushering her into a seat.

"How is he?" Gian asks.

"Stable," Melissa says. "They still don't know what caused the reaction, but his throat swelled up too much, and he couldn't breathe, which is why he ended up unconscious. They're getting a room ready for him right now. They said they'd call me when he can have visitors."

"That's good."

I nod, opening up my sandwich and taking a bite. It feels like swallowing a lump of dried glue, but I know I need to eat. On the wall beside us, the TV switches from a commercial to a newscast. A reporter comes on, dressed in a blouse and holding a microphone. She's out on the street, in front of the palace.

"Welcome back to Reneau One. I'm your host, Veronica Chambers, and we are counting down the hours until the royal wedding of Her Highness, Princess Aisling and the Duke of Belare, Brennan Lewis. We have a great show for you tonight, all about the wedding—from speculations of the princess' dress to the expected guest list…"

I choke on my sandwich. The wedding. In all the hustle and worry over Aaron, I'd somehow completely forgotten I was supposed to switch places with Chava tonight for my wedding tomorrow. I reach for my pocket, then remember that I'd given Chava's phone to Emilia for some stupid reason. I have no way to contact her or Florence.

Melissa and Gian are still talking, not having noticed my mini panic attack nor the newscast. I wonder if I might be able to sneak away, but I have no idea where I am in Reneau or how long it would take to get to the palace. I also have no way to get into the palace either; my original plan had been to call Florence to come get me and sneak me in, but now I don't have any phone numbers.

Melissa's phone rings, and she answers it, talking to whoever is on the other end. She hangs up after a moment, still serious but lighter.

"Aaron can have visitors," she says. "He's still asleep, but we can go up and be with him. Let's go." Melissa is on her feet in a flash. Gian stands as well and motions for me to get up. I glance down at my food, trying to stall. What if I say I'll stay down here to finish eating but leave for the palace? Chava can come back and claim she got lost, perhaps, or—

"You can bring your food up with you," Melissa says, grabbing my arm and hauling me up. "Let's go see your brother."

I deflate, defeated, but a small part of me is glad I'll be able to see Aaron one last time and make sure he's okay before I have to leave. I'll figure out some way to get back to the palace tonight. For now, I'll keep playing Chava.

# CHAPTER TWENTY-EIGHT
## CHAVA

WE ARE HALF AN HOUR INTO THE rehearsal dinner, and I have no idea how much longer it is going to go on. I've never known what really goes into a rehearsal dinner, but I thought that at some point it required *rehearsing* the *ceremony*. That is not the case for the palace, however.

I was taken to what Florence called the 'formal dining room' which was already filled with people I did not know. Some of them might have been at the ball; maybe all of them had been at the ball. I had no idea. But I was too nervous to be around the king or queen, and I did not know how to face Brennan, so I threw myself into the middle of conversations with strangers.

When the food had been served, I was brought to sit to the left of the king, opposite the queen who sat at his right. Of course, Brennan had been seated right next to me, but the first course was served, and I dug into the soup with a vigor I'd never given my mother's cooking.

The king hits his wine glass with a tiny spoon, the tone ringing throughout the room and quieting everyone. He stands, and everyone moves to stand with him, but he motions us down.

"Please, stay seated," he says. "I just want to give a speech to my daughter before the main course is served."

Everyone settles and looks toward him, though I feel eyes on me as well. I force myself to look up at the king, to not hide my face in my empty plate. The king smiles down at me kindly, the corners of his eyes wrinkling.

"My darling Aisling, I've both dreamed and dreaded of this moment for years," he begins. "Getting married brings you one step closer to becoming queen, to inheriting my crown, but it also takes you one step farther away from me."

He takes a breath and continues: "Every father wants the best for his children, especially for his daughter. We want to see you grow and thrive. We want to see you find someone who will love and care for you. And I know that your future is filled with light, and I can't wait to see how you shine that light on Vyctorya."

The king lifts his glass high. "To Her Highness, Princess Aisling!"

A chorus takes up the princess' name, but I can barely hear it. I can barely breathe. All I can think of is my father and what I've lost and what I'll never have. But I can't break, not now, not when I'm so close.

So I pick up my glass and take a drink of the expensive champagne and count down the minutes until I'm back in my bed at home, under my blue comforter and surrounded by nothing.

As soon as I get back to Aisling's room, I make a beeline for the phone and click on the contact for *Chava*. Maybe Emilia has gotten my phone back to her, and she can give me some answers. But the phone goes straight to voicemail.

*Hi, this is Chava. I'd really rather you send me a text, but if you have to, I guess leave a message.*

There's laughter in the background—my dad's.

*Dad, stop laughing! I'm trying to record here! Ignore him, just text me.*

There's a *beep* signaling the end of the message. I hang up, not bothering to leave a message.

I'd forgotten that my dad's laughter was on my voicemail. He'd stood over my shoulder as I recorded the message, fifteen years old with my new iPhone. I was going through that phase where I hated talking to people on the phone, so I always made people text me, which drove my mom crazy. My dad had found it hilarious.

That message was recorded a few months before he was diagnosed with cancer.

This is the first time I've heard his voice in so long— he hated being recorded, so we had next to no videos of him.

I call my phone again. Voicemail.

*Hi, this is Chava. I'd really rather you send me a text, but if you have to, I guess leave a message.*

My dad's laughter.

I close my eyes and listen, wishing he were here to help me through this.

# CHAPTER TWENTY-NINE
## AISLING

I WAKE UP DISORIENTED. I'M SITTING upright, and my neck is at an odd angle. There's a light beeping in the room, and a harsh glare hits me right in the eyes when I manage to squint them open. I shut them quickly and jerk my head out of the way. My body falls out of whatever I was sitting on, and I land hard on the linoleum floor.

"That was entertaining."

I look up to see Aaron lying in a hospital bed, hooked up to a bunch of machines. It all comes flooding back.

Aaron looks over at me and gives me a tight-lipped smile.

"Chava?" he asks. "Is it you?"

My heart sinks. "Uh, no, it's still me."

Aaron frowns. He looks down at his lap, and I'm struck by how small he looks in his bed, an IV attached to the back of his hand.

"How are you feeling?" I ask, standing up and walking over to him.

"I'm fine," he says, "but we have bigger problems."

I cock my head. "What?"

"The wedding?" He motions toward the TV mounted on the opposite wall. It's a news show, a blonde lady with a pearly white smile in a high-end dress in the middle of the screen. There's a small timer in the corner of the screen, ticking down the seconds until the royal wedding. My eyes go wide when I see it's almost ten o'clock. I'd stayed up well into the night with Melissa and finally collapsed into a chair around two in the morning, but I'd never dreamed that I would sleep for this long.

"Aaron!" I say. "Why didn't you wake me up?"

"Mama's been here," Aaron says. "She finally left to go get some breakfast after a lot of convincing. But you have to go *now*."

"You think I don't know that?" I exclaim. "But I'm on the opposite side of the city, I'll never get there in time!"

"I'll drive you," a voice says. Gian stands in the doorway, a set of keys in his hand. Aaron and I exchange a look of bewilderment.

"Uh, what?" Aaron asks. I still look at him wide-eyed. How are we going to play this off?

"I've known from the beginning, Your Highness," Gian says, taking a step farther into the room. "You're a dead ringer for my granddaughter, but you had something she hasn't had since her father died."

"And what was that?" I ask.

"Hope," Gian says. "I didn't know what the two of you were doing, but I let it play out. I thought maybe this would bring some of that life back into her, but I think it's gone on long enough."

"We were supposed to switch back yesterday, but Aaron—" I begin.

Gian cuts me off. "No time to waste. Let's get you to your wedding."

I nod and scramble to my feet. I make my way to Gian but pause at the foot of Aaron's bed.

"You're okay?" I ask.

"I'll be fine," he tells me.

"You know, it was nice to have a little brother, even for just a few days," I say.

Aaron smiles. "You still owe me a favor."

"Chava has my number." I turn back to Gian who waves his hand impatiently. He steps out of the room and into the hall. With one last wave to Aaron, I follow.

# CHAPTER THIRTY
# CHAVA

After the rehearsal dinner, Florence had dropped me off at Aisling's room and ordered me to sleep.

"It's going to be fine," she'd told me before shutting the door and closing me off from the outside world once more.

I'd paced the room the entire night. I was too keyed up to lay down, let alone try to close my eyes and sleep. By the time seven o'clock rolls around, I'm jittery yet exhausted, an awful combination.

The door to the room flies open without so much as a knock. Luka sweeps into the room, arm in front of him as if clearing the way.

"Are you ready for your big day, Your High—" Luka catches sight of me, and he falters. A hurricane of people flood in after him, swarming me immediately. No one seems to notice Luka's hesitation. A white woman with a platinum bob ushers me into the closet, handing me a silk robe and a white lace thong to change into. I change as quickly as possible, shrugging the robe on.

As soon as I'm decent, the woman grabs my arm and pulls me over to the vanity in Aisling's room. Luka stands behind the chair, talking in hushed tones to Florence who seems just as harried, a look I hadn't expected from her. She is dressed in a pale pink suit jacket and matching skirt, but her usual sleek ponytail is dotted with flyaways. When she and Luka turn to look at me, her eyes are bloodshot.

I sit down in the vanity chair and face the mirror. In the reflection, I see Luka take a deep breath, closing his eyes before a brilliant smile overtakes his face. He shoos away some of the lingering people, so that the only people near me are him and Florence. He steps closer to me and begins playing daintily with my hair.

"How are you doing?" Luka asks. His voice is cheery but low. To the outsider, it would seem as if he were asking a blushing bride about her nerves, but I'm not the blushing bride. I have no idea where the blushing bride is.

"I don't know what to do," I whisper.

"I've been calling the hospitals, but no one will tell me anything," Florence says.

"You still don't know which one A—" I cut myself off. I shouldn't say my brother's name "—*he* is at?"

Florence shakes her head. "I'm trying, but I have to be discreet."

My stomach is in knots. My hands grip the arms of the chair I sit in, the delicate skin of my fingers straining over the bones of my knuckles.

"I'm sure he's fine," Florence says. "You should be worrying about *yourself*."

"What happens if…" I trail off. Florence and Luka both know what I mean. They share a glance.

"It won't," Florence says firmly. Her hold on her phone tightens. "I'm going to go make some more calls. In the meantime, get her ready."

Luka seems uncertain. "Are you sure?"

Florence gestures around the room. The five people who'd followed Luka are spread out, each with their own individual task. Two are focused on a large case of makeup while the blonde lady who'd made me change earlier is talking into her headset.

"The wedding is at noon. We don't have a choice," Florence says to us. She walks out of the room without saying anything else. Luka turns to look at me in the mirror.

"Well," he says, "let's hope this isn't a complete and total disaster."

∼ ୧⟡୭ ∼

It takes Luka two hours to do my hair, much longer than the trial run the other day. But this time, he spends excruciating minutes on each curl, takes precise twists on each strand of hair that gets braided. At one point, the blonde woman comes over to complain, but he simply hushes her.

"You can't rush magic," he says. The woman huffs and leaves.

Once Luka is finally done with my hair, he calls over the makeup artist and her assistant. He stands slightly off to the side and watches carefully as the woman lines my eyes in black and paints my lips a soft shade of pink. He nitpicks each step, so that by the time she's done, it's been another hour.

The women pack up the makeup, sharing exasperated looks with each other, and head off to another corner of my room. Luka steps beside me once more, tilting my head this way and that to look at each angle in the mirror.

"What are you doing?" I ask.

"Trying to stall," Luka whispers. "But I don't think it's working. It's already ten o'clock, and Gracelynn will be here any minute."

As if on cue, Headset Lady appears, face still stern.

"The dress is here. Let's go, Your Highness. You need to get to the Bridal Suite."

I shoot Luka a panicked look, but he simply grimaces and helps me up.

"Let's go, people!" The blonde woman shouts orders as she clears the way, expecting me to follow in her wake. I slip on the pair of shoes placed in front of me and hurry after the woman, Luka close by my side.

"We're moving rooms?" My voice is high and stressed.

"She'll know where to find us," Luka tries to assure me, but his voice lacks his usual confidence. I swallow hard and try not to trip over my feet. The soles of these shoes are very slippery.

The doors to the Bridal Suite are open, and I'm ushered through them. They slam shut behind me, my heart dropping to my stomach with the *thud*. Gracelynn stands in the middle of the room, a large white garment bag hanging on the rack beside her.

Gracelynn beams at me. "Your Highness! You look beautiful!"

"Thank you," I say. I look around the room for Florence, but she's nowhere to be found. Headset Lady takes my arm and brings me to Gracelynn, who grabs the garment bag. She takes over for the woman, placing her arm around my shoulders and steering me behind the changing partition.

Gracelynn hangs the garment bag once more and unzips it, pulling out a handful of white fabric. The sight of it makes me want to throw up.

"Are you excited?" Gracelynn asks, her back to me. She's still working the dress out, fluffing parts of it and sighing dreamily.

"Uh…" I can't get words to form. They're stuck in my throat, worse than the time I'd choked on a fruit snack when I was in first grade. Gracelynn glances at me over her shoulder, giving me a soft smile. She turns around and places a hand on my arm.

"Don't be nervous, Your Highness," she says. "It'll all turn out."

I don't think it will, but I keep my thoughts to myself. Gracelynn reveals the full dress, just as fluffy and beautiful as it was a few days ago. I swallow hard. I shouldn't get in the dress. If I get in the dress, it's going to be really hard to get out of it once Aisling gets here because Aisling *will* be here.

Gracelynn senses my hesitation. "I know it's a big change, but you'll be fine. Now, hurry along."

She holds the dress out for me, and I carefully step into it. The skirt is pulled up to my hips. I slip off the robe so the bodice can be pulled up my chest, and then my arms go through the sleeves. Gracelynn smiles wistfully, a tear in her eye.

"Is everything all right?" I ask.

She sniffs a little, waving a hand. "Oh, I'm fine." She turns me around so she can start doing up the buttons that line my back. "You just... you remind me of someone I know, someone I care deeply about."

I can physically feel the color leave my face. I'm grateful she turned me around, grateful I'm face to face with a partition and no one else.

"Oh," I say, my voice small. "If you don't mind my asking, who?"

Gracelynn takes a deep breath. "My best friend."

I nearly whip around at that. *Mama?* I'd assumed she'd been talking about me, seeing as how I looked exactly like Aisling, but I was wrong. Before I can try to come up with something to say, Gracelynn speaks once more.

"I made her wedding dress, you know," she tells me quietly, as if it's a secret. "She designed it, but I spent months finding the perfect fabric and taking measurements and doing the tiniest stitches. It was beautiful, my favorite dress I've ever made. You can imagine my distress when her groom stepped on her train and tore it."

I smile. Mama had told that story about Papa a hundred times.

"I begged her to let me fix it, but she didn't want me to. She said… she said she liked that he'd left his mark on her, that every time she looked at it, she knew she would always think of him." Gracelynn's voice is thick. Her fingers, which had been moving with quick efficiency, have slowed on my back.

"Were—" I pause, trying to swallow what feels like a handful of marbles. "Were they happy together?"

Gracelynn's hands still completely. "The happiest."

My eyes are wet, and I fight to keep the tears at bay. The princess doesn't know the people Gracelynn is talking about; she doesn't know how their love story ended, so there's no reason for her to be sad.

But in all the time I'd spent pretending to get ready for this wedding—in all the time I'd mourned my father—it had never occurred to me that Papa would never get to see me married.

# CHAPTER THIRTY-ONE
# AISLING

The traffic is terrible. Cars are practically bumper to bumper as we try to make our way to the Palace. I watch the clock as the minutes tick by.

"We're never going to make it in time," I tell Gian. We've already had to drive from the complete opposite side of the city, taking over an hour with everyone flocking to the Palace.

"Don't worry," Gian tells me. He puts on his blinker and turns right, onto a street that is considerably less crowded. "There's a park I play chess at that has a great view of the Palace."

"So?" I ask.

"*So,*" Gian says, dragging the *o* in the word out. The edge of the park comes into view, and he slides into a parking spot, putting the car in park before shutting it off. "We're going to cut through it."

"That's never going to work!" I say. "How big is this park? How long does it take someone to walk it? How do we get from the park to the Palace?"

"It borders the forest you have in your backyard," Gian says.

I shake my head, still not getting it.

"It'll put us out at the servants' entrance. We can sneak in through there," he tells me. He unbuckles his seatbelt and gets out of the car, setting off into the park. I scramble after him.

"Wait! How are we going to sneak in?" I ask.

"I figured that was up to you," Gian says. "How were you going to sneak in originally?"

"I was supposed to be there *last night*, not *today*." There are so many more people around *today*. I saw reporters on practically every corner we passed. I'd slunk down in my seat and hid my face, worried they'd catch a glimpse and get the wrong impression. Even though, technically, it would be the right impression: the princess is skipping out on her *wedding*.

"We'll just have to take it one step at a time. Now, come on. We need to walk faster." Gian sets off at a brutal pace, one much faster than I'd anticipated. I stumble to catch up, but then we match step for step.

I try not to think too much as the palace starts to get closer, the towers and turrets growing taller and more looming. The entrance comes into view. There are several guards stationed around it, including one in the guard's station.

"What do we do?" I ask Gian, but he doesn't hesitate. He grabs my arm and marches me to the station.

The guards stare at me in varying states of confusion.

"Your Highness?" one asks.

"How did you get out of the castle?" the other asks.

"We don't have time for stories right now," I say. "I have a wedding to attend."

"Who's he?" the first guard asked, pointing at Gian.

"A relative," I lie. "Now, if you'll let us through?"

The guards let us pass by, some openly staring while others try to be covert about it. All of them are clearly shocked. I wonder if Florence can get to them before they mention anything to my parents' advisors or assistants.

I lead Gian over to the kitchen entrance and have him walk ahead of me so I can hide behind him. Everyone in the kitchen seems too busy to pay any attention to us, though, so we manage to make it through without incident.

It's once we're out of the kitchen when I start to worry. There aren't many good side hallways to get to my room, and I doubt we can just parade down the main hall. Even if my parents are already in the sanctuary, there are other guests who are bound to notice the crown princess wandering about in street clothes.

I open the door to the dining room and poke my head out. The hallway is clear, so I step out and motion for Gian to follow me. I turn to go to the left and hear a gasp.

Hope stands at the end of the hallway, arms full of linens. Her red hair is pulled back in a bun, but there are several strands that hang around her face. Her mouth is open in shock.

"Your Highness?" she asks.

"Uh…" I can't think of anything to say.

Hope takes a step back, and I worry she's going to run away, but then she motions with her head for us to come closer, so I do.

"Your Highness, I don't understand. I thought you were getting ready?" she asks.

"It's a long story," I say, "but I need to get to my room as quickly and quietly as possible. Can you help?"

Her eyes dart to Gian, curiosity written in her gaze, but she looks back at me and nods.

"Follow me," she says. She turns on her heel with almost militaristic precision and goes back the way she'd just came. She opens a small door a little further down the hall, revealing a thin set of stairs. Hope leads us up the stairs to the next floor, which reveals narrow hallways going in all directions.

"What is this?" I ask, hurrying after her.

"Shortcuts," she answers. She takes us up another flight of stairs, to what I assume is the third floor. "There's a door that's right around the corner from your room." She walks as quickly as she can. Behind me, I hear Gian breathing a little heavily but otherwise keeping up just fine. Hope stops at a door with a well-worn doorknob and opens it up. We all step out, and she ushers me around the corner. I sigh in relief when I see the door to my room.

"Okay," I say, turning to Gian. "I'll get Chava and bring her out here. Hope, can you help them get out of the palace?" Realization dawns on her face, but she nods anyway. I'm definitely going to owe her an explanation.

I open one of the doors to my room as quietly as I can, wondering if I can possibly sneak in near the walls and if it's even worth it, but then I see there's no point.

The room is empty.

# CHAPTER THIRTY-TWO
# CHAVA

I HAVE NO IDEA WHAT TIME it is. Outside, the day gets brighter and brighter. Inside, everyone is a flurry of movement while I sit on an upholstered armchair in the middle of the room—they're snowflakes in a blizzard, and I'm the eye of the storm.

Gracelynn comes over to check on me every ten minutes or so to mess with the dress, but other than that, I'm mostly left alone. I get side eyes and giggles, but no one speaks to me until finally, the double doors open, and Luka glides in. He zeroes in on me, and I breathe a sigh of relief at his familiar face.

"What's happening?" I whisper when he gets close enough. He moves behind me, pulling at the stray curls he'd left down to frame my face.

"We can't find her," Luka tells me quietly.

I feel like I might throw up.

"What do you mean you can't find her?" I demand. "How many goddamn hospitals are there in this city?"

"Florence had a lead, but then the king and queen called her over and haven't left her alone since. She's supposed to sit in a place of honor beside them during the ceremony. It was a surprise and a 'thank you' for taking care of the princess for all these years."

"How nice." It is not nice.

"The king is coming to collect you shortly," Luka says.

There's a ball in my stomach, threads of worry and fear and despair all tangled together. I swallow hard. "What do I do?"

"You just have to go with it."

"*Go with it?*" My voice is too loud, the last word pitching at a volume that feels like only dogs can hear. There is a momentary pause where every person in the room stares at me. I stare back, completely frozen.

"Jitters," Luka says, waving a hand. It takes a moment, and what I assume is a hard look from Luka, for the room to get back in motion.

"I can't get married," I whisper harshly. "Are you insane? I'm only eighteen!"

"The *princess* is getting married," Luka says, his words barely audible. "It'll be okay."

There's a knock on the door. Headset Lady hurries to the door and cracks it open. She descends into a curtsy, and soon everyone else is doing the exact same. The king steps into the room, eyes scanning every face before landing on mine. He gives a small, proud smile and nods his head.

*It's not okay, it's not okay, it's not okay.*

Before I can register what's happening, Luka has pulled me up, and Gracelynn has rushed over to pick at the dress some more. Headset Lady motions for me to get to the doorway, and I take robotic steps, hoping the terror I feel isn't written all over my face.

The king smiles down at me and holds his arm out. Shaking slightly, I loop my arm through his.

"Let's go, people," Headset Lady orders. Two maids come to lift the train off the ground, and the king begins to lead me down the hallway. I do my best to take deep, steady breaths so I don't hyperventilate. Beside me, the king chuckles.

"Nervous?" he asks.

I can barely look at him out of the corner of my eye.

"I was, too," he says. "And so was your mother. But it all worked out. We became a family, didn't we?"

"Mmhmm," I manage to squeak out.

Up ahead, I can see several people gathered around a large set of mahogany doors. The doors to the sanctuary.

It's so close.

I'm going to throw up.

"Hey." The king stops walking. He puts his hands on my shoulders and turns me to face him. "I know we've pushed you to do this, but… but if you're really not ready, we can wait."

"What?" The word is a whisper.

"I love you, Aisling, and I would do anything for you," he tells me. "Say the word, and it's off. We'll figure something out."

Headset Lady, who'd gone ahead to the doors, looks over at us. "One minute," she says.

"Aisling?" the king asks.

"I want to get married," I say. The words leave a bad taste in my mouth. But Aisling had told me her duty, and I was going to follow it through.

The king smiles. "All right." He fixes my hand through his arm once more and leads me to the doors. They swing open, and ceremonial music attacks my ears. Inside the sanctuary, everybody stands up in the pews.

The king takes the first step forward, and I stumble after him. Ahead, at the end of the aisle, I see Brennan dressed in an all black tuxedo, a crisp white shirt peeking out underneath the jacket.

When is Aisling going to get here? Will we have time to switch out at some point during the day? Am I going to have to *consummate* the marriage? Is that something they still do?

Fuck, fuck, fuck, I hadn't even thought of that.

And then, the music stops. There are gasps. All eyes are at the back of the church. I turn around.

Aisling's there.

# CHAPTER THIRTY-THREE
# AISLING

I AM THE MOST UNDERDRESSED person at this wedding, which is kind of funny considering I'm supposed to be the best dressed. Instead, that's Chava, standing in the middle of the aisle. She's let go of my father's arm and taken a step away from him. I look to my father to see his eyes trained on me, his face pale.

Behind me, a blonde lady in a headset is completely frozen. So is everyone else around her. Gian and Hope are a few steps away, out of sight of everyone in the sanctuary.

I, however, am in full view.

"Um, hello?" I say. I expect everyone to erupt at once, but still, no one speaks. I take a few steps further down the aisle, closer to Chava and my father.

"What—who are you?" Dad demands.

"It's me, Dad," I say. I pull out my emergency button, still on a chain around my neck. I hope Florence is proud to see that I never took it off.

Dad looks over at Chava. "Then who is…?"

I get close enough that I can loop my arm through Chava's and pull her beside me. I got her into this mess, the least that I can do is protect her.

"This is Chava," I say. "She's from America." It's probably not the best explanation, but it was the first thing that came to mind.

"Hi," Chava says, waving a little. Mum has now appeared beside Dad, her hand at her heart as she stares at us with wide eyes. "You… have a lovely home?"

"What is going on?" Mum asks, her voice faint.

"I met Chava last week, and I convinced her to switch places with me," I tell them. I'm very aware of the audience I have, both in the sanctuary and on television. This probably isn't the best place to have this conversation, but what else can I do?

"I don't understand," Mum says. "Why?"

"I don't want to get married," I say. I crane my head around my parents to see the duke still at the altar, his expression shell-shocked. "No offense to you, but you're not exactly my type."

"What are you doing?" Chava hisses.

I think about what Emilia had said to me, and I think about my speech at the memorial, about taking risks.

"Being myself," I tell Chava. Then, I turn to my parents. "I don't like men."

There's a gasp, almost as if it was rehearsed.

I continue on. "I'm a lesbian."

My parents stare at me, their expressions unchanged, as if I'd broken something in their brains.

"I'm sorry if that makes me less perfect to you," I say, "but I can't live my life pretending to be someone I'm not. I can't marry someone I will never love, no matter how nice and charming and handsome he is. I don't know what this means for you, but I know that for me, this means taking back a little freedom that I've given up."

Mum and Dad still say nothing. I look around at the impromptu audience I have, seeing the same expression of shock written on everyone's faces. A seed of doubt plants itself in my chest. Maybe this was too much too soon. Maybe I hadn't thought it out as much as I should have.

Let's be honest—I didn't think about this at all.

But when I look back at my parents, my grandmother is there.

My mother is a carbon copy of her mother. And even if Nani has a few more wrinkles than she once did, she's still one of the most beautiful people I've ever seen. She steps forward and cups my cheek.

"My darling girl," she says. "My darling, *brave* girl, there is nothing you could do to make you less perfect in my eyes." She pulls me forward and wraps me in her embrace.

"I didn't know you would be here," I say, clinging to her for dear life.

"And miss my granddaughter's wedding? Never," Nani says. "Though, I suppose the wedding is off, wouldn't you agree?" She directs this to my parents. Mum has seemingly unfrozen. Her eyes are now filled with tears.

"Yes, of course," she says. "Aisling, I'm so sorry." She brings her arms around me, too, and I melt into her.

"You didn't know," I tell her.

"No," she agrees, "but I should have. I should have been there for you."

I pull back. "I just need you now."

Mum nods, but her tears overtake her, and she can't say anything else. Dad is still silent, but he reaches out and brushes a strand of hair behind my ear, and I know that we'll be okay.

"So, can I… go?" Chava asks. I start. I'd forgotten she was there.

"I mean, I'll change out of the dress, but like…" Chava continues, pointing over her shoulder with her thumb.

"Your grandfather is here," I tell her.

Chava's brow furrows. "Dada?"

Gian pokes his head around the door before stepping into the sanctuary. He smiles at Chava, but when he turns to me, he freezes.

Beside me, Nani gasps. "Gian?"

He takes a step closer. "Ishara?"

Chava and I look at each other, utterly confused. Now I know how the wedding guests feel.

Nani rushes at Gian before we can say anything and throws her arms around his neck. He wraps his arms around her as well, both of them laughing and crying.

"Nani, what—" I begin, but she cuts me off.

"My baby brother, alive and well," she says, holding his face between her hands. "I thought of you every single day, do you know that? I never stopped missing you."

"I never stopped missing you either," Gian says, hugging her.

Mum places a hand on my shoulder. "Mother?" she asks.

Nani turns to face us, smiling sadly. "A year after my marriage, my younger brother was arranged in a marriage, but instead of going through with it, he'd run away from India. I was heartbroken, but I was never able to find my brother. Until now." She turns back to Gian, laughing.

"We're related?" I say to Chava. It's both a statement and a question.

"What?" Chava asks.

"We're related," I say again.

"Huh." Chava purses her lips. "Well, that explains a lot."

# CHAPTER THIRTY-FOUR
## CHAVA

Despite my worry, the king and queen do not have me thrown in the dungeons. I don't know their exact thoughts on me, but I'm not sure they know either. Right now, I'm pretty sure the only thing on their brains is shock.

Florence appears in the mess of the audience to escort me out of the sanctuary to change, leaving Aisling with her parents and Dada with his long lost sister. Florence leads me back to Aisling's room.

"Are you going to be all right?" I ask.

Florence shrugs. "I don't know."

"I'm so sorry," I say.

"I'm not," Florence assures me. "Even if I do get fired, Aisling came out. She gets to be herself, and that's all I wanted for her."

"You're a good friend," I say. "And hey, if the palace doesn't end up working out, I'm sure Gracelynn would gladly hire you on. She's been wanting to expand."

Florence laughs. "Speaking of Gracelynn, I should probably go find her. I'll try to do some damage control for you."

I wince. "That would be appreciated."

"I'll let you get changed," Florence says. I step inside the room, and Florence shuts the door. I go into Aisling's closet to get some normal clothes—I'll give them back to her when she gives mine to me—and then walk over to the partition. I kick off the shoes and carefully remove the tiara from my head. A piece of the filigree gets caught in my hair, and it takes me a minute to untangle it. Once the strands are free, I set the crown carefully on a cushion and move my attention to the dress. That's when I remember the buttons.

"Shit," I whisper. I hurry over to the door and open it, hoping to catch Florence. "Florence, the buttons—" I cut myself off. Brennan stands on the other side of the door. He's lost his jacket, and his sleeves are rolled up to his elbows. The bowtie is loose and hanging lifelessly around his neck, and his hair, which had been carefully styled, is now an array of curls.

"Need some help?" he asks.

I look around, desperate for literally any other person, but I find no one. I swallow hard and look back at Brennan.

"Uh, please," I say. I step back and let him inside the room. We go over to the partition, and I turn my back to him. Gently, he sets his hands on my shoulders then slides them to the first button. He works silently, and his fingers fumble every once in a while.

"How long?" Brennan asks. I don't have to ask him what he means.

"The entire time," I say.

He lets out a breath that fans over the back of my neck. I squeeze my eyes shut, horrified to find they burn. I feel little drops of water against my lashes.

"I never wanted to hurt you," I say. "You weren't supposed to find out." His hands are at my mid-back now, and my skin prickles at the onslaught of cold air.

"Is that supposed to make me feel better?" he asks.

"I don't know," I say. He finishes with the buttons and steps to the other side of the partition. I slide out of the dress, very aware of the fact that he is on the other side, and quickly pull on the leggings and shirt I'd taken.

"Was any of it real?" Brennan asks. I pause in the process of pulling on a sock. I step out and look at him, though I keep my hands on the partition.

"Very real," I say.

Brennan lets out a sad laugh. "I don't even know your name."

"Chava," I tell him. "Chava Burke. I moved to Vyctorya about a year ago with my mother and brother."

"And your father?" Brennan asks, but I know that he knows the answer. I just shake my head.

"I'm sorry," he says.

"Me too," I say. "It hurts a lot, still, which is why I can't give you what I want to."

"I understand," Brennan says quietly. We stand there for a moment in silence. Then, "Can you give me your phone number?"

My eyes flick to his. Surprise is written on his face, like he hadn't expected himself to say that either.

"Yeah," I say, smiling, "I'd like that."

Dada is too busy catching up with his sister, so Florence arranges for a car to take me to the hospital. I quickly thank the driver when we arrive and then hurry into the building. The receptionist stares at me as I walk up to the desk, which is fair, considering I'd just been on television and my hair and makeup are still done up like a bride.

"What room is Aaron Burke staying in?" I ask her.

"307," she tells me.

"Thanks."

I take the elevator up to the third floor and quickly find Room 307. The door is closed, so I pause to take a breath before knocking. The door flies open, and Mama stares at me.

"Hi," I say. She pulls me inside, shutting the door behind us. Then, before I can say anything else, she crushes me into a hug.

"I saw," she says. "And Aaron told me everything."

I look over my shoulder to see Aaron sitting up in bed, an IV attached to his wrist and a monitor on his pointer finger.

"I'm so sorry," I say to them. "It was just… it was too much."

"I know," Mama says, petting my hair. "I have so much to say to you. We'll do better. All of us."

She pulls back after a moment and looks at me. "So?"

"So what?" I'm nervous. Is she going to ask about Brennan? What do I say?

"How was the interview with the dean?" she asks.

Shit. I'd completely forgotten about that. I fumble around in my pockets for my phone, looking at my email. At the top, there's a message from Purdue, sent at 4:32 last night. I click on it.

*Dear Chava Burke,*

*We are pleased to inform you of your admission to the Fall semester at Purdue University in West Lafayette, IN. The dean was impressed with your past work as well as your interview…*

There's more to the letter, more words, more jargon, but all I can do is stare at the first line.

"I got in," I whisper. "I got in!"

Mama cheers and wraps me in a hug, pulling me over to Aaron, so he can join as well. I can't believe it. I thought I'd screwed my interview up for sure, but the dean liked it.

"When do you leave?" Mama asks.

I falter. "Leave?"

"For Indiana?" Mama prompts.

I sit down on the edge of Aaron's bed. "I don't know."

"Chava?"

"I already left once," I say. "I feel bad doing it again."

"This is your dream, sweetheart," Mama says. "You can't give that up." Tears that had threatened to overflow for so long spill over at the term of endearment. I can't remember the last time my mother called me that. I lean against her shoulder and cry—ugly, choking sobs. Mama strokes my hair, shushing me.

"Your Papa would be so proud of you," she tells me.

And for once, since the moment he died, I believe he would be.

# EPILOGUE
# AISLING

I PACE MY ROOM, FINGERS playing with each other. Florence stands at the door, arms crossed and watching me with an amused expression on her face.

"What?" I snap, then wince at my snappishness.

"It's going to be fine," she tells me.

"You don't know that," I whine.

"She agreed to come, didn't she?" Florence says.

She has a point.

It's been a few days since the wedding. The duke has gone back to Belare, apparently with Chava's phone number, leaving me with a story I needed to get caught up on. Nani was still here, and either had Gian visiting at the palace or was traveling to Chava's house to see him there. Mum had even tagged along once, in part to meet her uncle and in part to see where I had stayed for nearly a week. Everything was going better than I had expected.

Except I hadn't heard from Emilia.

I'd finally confessed to Chava that I'd grown feelings for her ex-girlfriend, but instead of being mad, she'd smiled and come up with this plan—inviting Emilia to the palace.

And now, I'm waiting for Emilia to show up; she should have been here seven minutes ago.

"There was probably traffic," Florence assures me.

"No, she hates me, and she doesn't want to see me, so she's canceled," I say.

"The driver would have called me to tell me that no one showed up," she says.

*Knock, knock.*

I freeze, then straighten up. I pull my hair over my shoulder only for it to fall back into place. It's still too short for me to do that.

Florence opens the door, and there Emilia stands. She wears a blue sundress and has a worn brown bag that she clutches the strap of.

"Did no one bring you up?" I ask when I don't see anyone around her.

"No, they did," Emilia says, stepping inside. "They just kind of knocked and dashed for some reason."

"Oh," I say. Florence looks at me, then at Emilia, then back at me.

"Well, I have some work that needs to be done. Just let me know when Emilia wants to leave, and I'll have a driver take her home," Florence says.

I make a face at her, a *please don't leave me alone* face, but she simply smirks at me and leaves. Emilia stands awkwardly in the doorway.

"Tea?" I ask, motioning over to my sitting area where a tray of tea and biscuits are waiting for us.

"Sure," Emilia says. She comes over and sits on the couch. I sit across from her and go about making the teacups. "So, what did you want to talk about?"

My hand shakes, and the tea spills a little. Emilia reaches forward to grab a napkin and mop up the spill. Carefully, I set the pot down and sit back, hands folded in my lap.

"Um, you see, I, uh, well—" I stammer.

"I thought princesses were supposed to be well-spoken," Emilia teases.

I look up, relieved at her joke. It makes me more confident.

"I wanted to apologize for tricking you," I say. "That was never my intention."

"Then what was your intention?" Emilia asks.

"To be normal," I say. "I never thought I'd meet you. If I had, I would have recalibrated. I would have accounted for the fact that I might… that I might… feel for someone the way I'd never felt before."

I take a deep breath. "Emilia, I know the time we spent together probably feels cheap and fake, but to me, it was everything. It was real. I promise you that. And I understand if you never want to see me again, but I just… I can't go on without telling you how I feel."

I realize that I've been staring at my lap this whole time, my knuckles bloodless. I force myself to look up. Emilia looks at me softly, a slight smile on her lips.

"I won't lie," she says. "I didn't like being tricked. I thought I was just falling back in love with someone I knew. I never knew I was falling for someone I'd never met."

My heart leaps at her words.

"I'm hesitant," Emilia continues. "I don't want to be your trial and error. I don't want to give my heart to someone who's scared to give me theirs."

"I'm not scared anymore," I tell her. To prove my point, I get up and sit next to her, our bare knees touching. Emilia looks down and then back up. She grabs my hand and laces her fingers with mine.

"I won't be your trial and error," she repeats, "but I will be your first."

"I never thought I'd get to have a first," I admit.

Emilia smiles. She brings her hand to my face, her thumb brushing my cheek lightly. Slowly, she leans forward and kisses me. My breath catches, and she pulls back a little.

"Did I—?" she begins.

I press my lips against hers, cutting her off.

I don't know what I expected a kiss to be like, but it's better than anything I could have dreamed up. It's soft and sweet and wonderful, and when she cups my face in her hands, I feel as if I could burst.

I lock this moment in my mind, never wanting to forget it.

# — THE END —

# ACKNOWLEDGMENTS

There are many people to thank in regards to Princess and the Pauper. First, if it weren't for Emerson College and my incredible thesis committee, Anna Burke and Katie Williams, this book would not exist. I was going through a really hard time when I wrote this in 2021-2022, and Anna was truly my biggest supporter as my thesis chair, so thank you dearly.

I'd like to thank everyone at Wild Ink Publishing, especially Abigail Wild. I am completely new to the publishing world, and my first conversation with Abby, when she offered to publish my book, was both comforting and exciting.

I'd like to thank my incredible editor, Andie Smith, for working with me and helping make my book the best it could possibly be. The turnaround time was quick, but I'm proud of what I've put out into the world, and it wouldn't have been possible without Andie's help.

I'd like to thank the community I've built in Hattiesburg, MS at the University of Southern Mississippi, Center for Writers. I received my offer for Princess and the Pauper while at USM, and the guidance and support I've received from the faculty as well as the friends I've made has been instrumental.

Finally, I'd like to thank some of the most special people in my life. I'd like to thank my mother, my first supporter, someone who always believed in me when I didn't necessarily believe in myself. I'd like to thank all of my friends, both old and new, for supporting me and lifting me up. And I'd like to thank my best friend, Carol—I'm so glad we wrote that awful book our senior year of high school, and I hope this one makes you proud.

## ABOUT ISABELLE KELLY

Isabelle Kelly received her degree in English Literature from Ball State University and her MFA in Popular Fiction and Publishing from Emerson College. Her short story, "The Ones Left Behind," was published in the inaugural edition of *Page Turner Magazine*. When not reading or writing, Isabelle enjoys playing the piano, cake decorating, and traveling. Currently, she resides in southern Mississippi with her cat, Jane Bennet, pursuing her PhD in English – Creative Writing at the University of Southern Mississippi, Center for Writers.

www.ingramcontent.com/pod-product-compliance
Lightning Source LLC
Chambersburg PA
CBHW031209310726
48969CB00001B/274